SLEEPING BEASTY

WOLF SHIFTER FAIRY TALE RETELLINGS
BOOK TWO

BELLA MOONDRAGON

For Mr. K. even though you were kind of weird.

CONTENTS

PRINCESS MAXIANA

Max

I slip further into the milky, rose scented water of my bath, closing my eyes against the soft pitter-patter of Annabel's slippers as she searches for me in what sounds like desperation. Her exaggerated sigh and mumbles bring a smile to my face, but I sink under water until I'm totally submerged, my hair floating on the surface.

I hear her gasp and cry out as she rushes to the tub, but I burst from the water, laughing as I brush my wet hair from my face.

"You scared me to death!" Annabel snaps, her cheeks going a deep, rosy pink. "Goddess, Max, I thought you'd drowned!"

"You think I'd be dumb enough to do that on the day of my own ball?" I slide to the side, resting my arms on the rim of the tub, smirking up at my lady-in-waiting–my only real friend, if I'm being honest. Annabel scowls as she moves through the spacious bathroom before whirling and resting her hip against the counter, her arms crossed and lower lip curled downward as she pouts.

"Oh, please, Anna," I yawn. "You act like you've never had fun a day in your life."

"That makes two of us," she replies curtly, arching a perfect manicured dark brow. "Have you been in here the whole time? I've been looking for you for ages. We need to start getting you ready."

I look up at the skylight over the bathtub, at the crystal clear, late afternoon sky. "We still have hours, don't we?"

"Yes, but guests are already arriving, and your father will call for you at sunset, and..." She looks me over, honing in on my damp hair. "I need to fix your hair, and do your makeup, get you into that stunning but complicated gown–"

"We have time for all of that. Don't you worry." I rise from the tub, ignoring her blush as she turns toward the counter, her arm flailing blindly for a towel.

I pluck it from her hand and wrap myself up before padding into my bedroom to find the robe I forgot to bring into the bathroom with me. Annabel huffs about the trail of water I'm leaving behind, and normally I wouldn't be so careless, but... I feel *it*. I didn't think I would. All the books I've read made it sound like coming into my wolf powers–my ability to shift, my heightened senses of sight, sound, and smell–would be abrupt, like being shocked the second the sun goes down on the eve of my twenty-first birthday.

I woke up feeling different, however. Even stroking my fingers across the pale pink satin sheets that line the gargantuan white, four-poster bed in the center of my gilded room had my body humming to life, like a simple touch is now too sensitive. I could hear the whispered voices of the maids as they scurried around the castle clear as day. My breakfast tasted... *incredible*. Better than anything I've ever eaten before, and I've eaten the same plate of fruit with eggs and toast every day for the past several years.

I'm changing. It's happening.

I drop the towel and shrug my arms into my robe, whirling toward Annabel. My wet hair sprays water everywhere, but I'm beyond caring. Annabel winces, thumbing a few drops of water from her cheeks, and gracefully folds her arms under her chest as she looks me up, and down, trying to decide where to begin.

She sighs and unravels her arms. "Hair first, I think. That'll take the longest."

I grin at her, choking back a girlish squeal as she waves me to my vanity. She cracks open a window, using the breeze to speed up the drying as she brushes, and brushes, my hair until it shines like golden silk.

"What color of fur do you think I'll have?" I ask, catching her eyes in the mirror.

She smiles softly to herself as she winds my now dry hair into thick braids. "Gold, for sure. Just like your mother."

"But aren't golden wolves rare?"

"They are. I've never seen one. But who knows… maybe the rumors are true, and you'll be the first golden wolf born in a generation." Annabel's a few years older than me at twenty-five. She can shift. She could do so right now, tearing through her simple gray dress and starch-white apron, but she's classy and quiet, always preferring order over playfulness.

"What color is your fur again?"

"A tawny brown, like most wolves," she smiles, weaving the braids together into a long, thick plait down my back.

I drum my fingers on the vanity as she continues doing my hair, pressing pearl clips along the plait until my hair glimmers like jewels spread out on a golden stretch of satin. She brushes my cheeks with blush and swipes glimmering peach eyeshadow over my eyelids with practiced grace. Annabel came to live and work at the castle five years ago, and I've been her little doll ever since.

Within the hour I look more like a princess and less like a swamp creature, much to Annabel's delight.

I smooth my hand over the shimmery pink fabric of the gorgeous gown my father had made for the occasion–my twenty-first birthday, the day my life changes forever. Annabel's eye's drift over the dress, inspecting the drop waist and sweetheart neckline before adjusting the tight bodice with inlaid boning. My waist is pinched and on full display in the gown, which is a far cry from the simple, flowy dresses I wear day to day, but this is a special occasion and requires a very special gown, indeed.

But my maid's expression shifts, her soft brown eyes going glassy with worry. "What's the matter?" I ask, but she shakes her head, pressing her lips into a tight smile.

"We're just a little early. We have to wait." She glances at the windows, at the late afternoon sky. The sun is just starting to set, and she sighs at the sight, turning away from me while wringing her hands.

"Maybe you can just… take me to the ball early? I don't understand why I have to wait. I can hear the music coming from downstairs already. I'll have missed half of my own ball by the time–"

"It's customary, Princess," she says formally.

I startle, used to her calling me Max–or Maxiana. She only calls me Princess if she's upset with me for something.

Her eyes lower to the ground. "Max, your father has a plan to bring you out and show you off to the court once the sun sets and the full moon rises. You knew that. You've known that for months now. We have to follow the schedule." She glances at the window again, her cheeks flaring a deep red. I swear on the Moon Goddess I see glimmers of sweat breaking out along her neat hairline.

"You don't need to be so nervous, Annabel. Look at me! You made me the most beautiful woman in all of Vaeloria, let alone the prettiest wolf of the Ebonclaw pack."

Her tight, anxious smiles twitches into something warm. "Thank you, Max."

A sharp knock on my bedroom door steals her attention. With a huff, she whirls as a maid pops her head in, rasping, "Annabel, we need your help."

Annabel glances at me before asking sharply, "With what? I'm supposed to stay with the princess–"

"One of the guards has been sneaking wine and is terribly drunk. He's slumped in one of the hallways off the ballroom. I can't move him, and the other guards won't help. They're not allowed to leave their posts."

Annabel sighs, wringing her hands again to the point that her knuckles turn a ghostly white. "Fine. But quickly, all right? Princess Maxiana, stay here, I'll be back in a moment." She hurries away, slipping through the door and closing it with a soft click.

Silence swells. I turn toward the full length mirror, smoothing the shimmering, scale-like jewels hanging like teardrops from my gown. The jewels were plucked from a gown my mother used to wear–my father's favorite in her extensive collection. Her clothes and jewels are all we have left of her besides her portrait in the library–one of the only rooms I've ever been allowed to explore. I look like her, with our shared thick, golden hair full of soft, gentle waves. She was a tall woman from what I've been told–graceful and slender, moving like water through a trickling stream. Her eyes were blue, like mine. A radiant, sparkling blue. Her name was Aurora. She came from a land far away, and she loved us.

"I wish you were here," I whisper into the silence. I wish I remembered her, but I was so, so young when she died that I have no memories whatsoever. Well, just one, I think. I hum that strange tune–the music I can't get out of my head. Music I'm sure I made up during my childhood trapped within the walls of this castle.

I've never been beyond the front gate. I've never walked through the village of Ebonclaw or the rolling woodlands of Vaeloria beyond. I've never been seen by the public, my own people.

But tonight, that changes.

Maybe I'll even find my mate. Wouldn't that be amazing?

I pace the room, running my fingertips over bottles of perfume and down the spines of books. I dream about *him* sometimes, my mate. At least, I think it's him. Who else could it be? Who else's hands would be drawing up my sides, caressing my bare, starlit skin? Who else could possibly whisper the most beautiful praise in my ear while his hands drift upward to cup my breasts? In my dreams, he cages me against his chest while pointing at the stars dancing across the sky before kissing me tenderly, then deeply, those kisses traveling down my stomach until he disappears between my thighs.

I've never seen his face. His image is a haze, shadowed by darkness, and anytime we're together, it's always at night. Always under the stars.

I shiver, chuckling softly as I close my eyes and try to banish the shockingly vivid dreams. They've been coming more often now, sometimes nightly, like he's calling out to me through the bond I'll recognize *tonight*. Maybe he's in the ballroom right now, waiting for me.

Maybe he already knows.

I hum the tune again as my fingers drift over the piano in the corner of my room—my favorite thing in the world. I love to play. I love to sing and dance and just... be free—as free as I can be in this castle.

The door opens on a soft breeze tinted with the smell of... ozone, like a storm rolling toward the village.

"Princess Maxiana? Are you ready? I'm here to fetch you for the ball."

I turn to the unfamiliar voice and stare at the young maid. She's tall, with sleek, black hair and a devastating kind of beauty. Her eyes are a vivid... green—but a shade I've never seen before.

I don't recognize her at all, and the maids and servants of this castle have been my only company for my entire life.

"Who are you?"

"Morgan, your grace," she says with a smile and practiced curtsy. She's wearing the uniform of the maids. That soft gray dress and apron. "I'm new. I'm afraid we haven't had a chance to formally meet, but your father sent me directly."

"Where's Annabel?" I ask a bit skeptically, stepping toward her.

"She's busy. She's been called away but told me where to find you."

"Oh, well..." I look toward the window. The sun hasn't set. But the sunset is... starting, at least. Perhaps father decided to bring me out early, too excited to wait any longer. He's the Alpha King of Ebonclaw and has only one child—me. He dotes on me, loves me tenderly and wholly. He calls me the sky that hangs the moon for him.

"Father's excited, isn't he?" I grin, excitement bubbling through my body. "Fine, let's go. I'm just dying to dance."

Her smile is feline, her eyes creasing as she holds open the door. I step into the hallway, breathing in deeply the scent of wine and candles creeping from the ballroom downstairs.

Music and revelry drift through the air, beckoning me with every stroke of the bow across the strings of a violin

"Hurry now, Your Grace. We don't have much time," she says, waving me along.

"Time for what?" I laugh, rushing down the hallway with her, but... something feels off. Father had every able bodied warrior stationed at the castle tonight for this party, but they're nowhere to be seen in the winding hallways of cream-colored stone and stained glass.

"This way," she says, opening a door I... I don't remember being there.

"What's this?" I ask, confused, as she steps into the darkness.

"A gift," she says. "Come, we have to hurry. Your father insisted you open it before the sun fully sets."

"A gift?" My fingers tingle. I do love gifts...

"A gift your mother left for you, for your twenty-first birthday." She grins wildly, beckoning me to follow. I rush up a spiraling stone staircase behind, laughing with the maid–with Morgan. I love new friends. "Come now, can you hear it? The music?"

"What music?" I giggle, but when my breath runs out I hear... *that song*. That tune I always hum. The song I thought I made up.

I would stop to listen, but Morgan takes my hand, tugging me up each step as the music laces through my body, curling around my bones and settling deep in my soul. I feel overcome, my vision blurring as light trickles down the steps–eerie, vivid green light. Haven't I just seen something that same color?

We reach the top of the stairs. A small, snug bedroom comes into view, everything... everything smells like roses and... rain. A four-poster bed rests in the center of the room draped in lace, and on the cushions rests a golden box, the lid propped open, with music flowing from it.

A golden rose spins in its center to the tune, its golden thorns catching the last light of sunset. I'm drawn to it, my fingers outstretched.

"Yes, girl," Morgan rasps behind me. "Touch it."

I can't stop myself. Green light floods the room, filling my vision. All I can see is the rose and all I hear is the music as my pointer finger stretches. I just... want to feel it–the cold metal–the gift left by a mother I never knew but desperately miss.

The music rushes through my ears as my finger brushes over a single, golden thorn.

"Yes... yes... do it!"

"MAXIANA!" Annabel screams my name as the thorn bites into my skin. The room spins before going an inky, dark, black.

KING KAEL

Kael

I CROSS INTO THE SHADOWS OF A CAVERNOUS, ECHOING PALACE. RAIN slips down the dark stone walls from tunnels funneling upward toward breaks in the mountain that guards the castle built against *and* within its depths. I adjust my cuffs, smoothing the dark, intricate fabric of my black jacket inlaid with shimmering, polished beads of obsidian, and look up, facing the twisting onyx columns as I cross into the sanctum–the very center of the dilapidated castle.

Four men wait in silence, their eyes scanning and inspecting me as I approach. My footsteps carry, thundering through the wide, open space. The air is damp and scented with ozone as a storm of epic proportions rages overhead, casting the steep, unforgiving mountain-scape in ribbons of electric blue, just visible through the holes in the ceiling.

I fucking hate this place.

"King Kael," calls a man in the center of the group, giving me a sharp, shallow nod of his head.

"King Titus," I reply with little fanfare, returning his nod with one of my own.

The other men grumble their greetings, shifting in their finery like they're uncomfortable, and like me, would rather be anywhere else. Thunder booms overhead, followed by more brilliant stripes of lightning that cuts through the warmth glowing from the candlelit chandelier trembling two stories above our heads.

I come to a stop a comfortable distance away from the other men—the other kings. I can't remember the last time we were called together like this. Our kingdoms aren't… friendly with one another, to say the least.

My hands curl into fists at my side before I tuck them behind my back, waiting for someone, anyone, to start talking.

Every man in the room is looking at me, however.

"Titus," I say, rolling my neck and fixing the elderly, yet spry and as dangerous as ever, man a look dripping with boredom. "Would you care to explain why you've called this meeting? This meeting in the dead of night, I might add?"

Titus's wide, black eyes narrow on mine, but his mouth twitches into a slightly teasing smile as he replies, "A council of the kings was simply overdue."

"What could we possibly have to discuss?" King Ashton says with marked sarcasm.

I bite the inside of my cheek to stop from smiling. I've always liked him, especially when he's face to face with Titus. King Ashton of Terminus, a mountain range not far from this ancient, normally empty fortress, is young, like me. His windswept, icy blond locks curl around his pointed ears as he paces away from the group, casting a cat-like glare at Titus.

Titus is an elder. *The* elder, our Alpha King, so to speak, if our kind ever decided to revert back to the old ways. I find it hard to believe that would ever happen, given how little of us there are left.

In another time, we'd be kneeling in his presence, not scowling with talons drawn. Times have changed. Times are hard. Times are only getting harder as the minutes tick by, spent here, wasted in the presence of King Titus of Rageworn Mountain, the boot-licking simp of Queen Morgathra and her coven of displaced witches, those banished from Hexeton by the witch queen Maeve, the guardian of that kingdom.

King Henrick of Hightower glances between me and Ashton. I haven't seen him in ten years, at least. He's middle-aged for our kind. His advancing years show on his face in lines that gather around his eyes as he narrows his gaze on Titus, licking his lips before saying, "If there was nothing to discuss, I'm leaving. I won't stand here and be taunted."

Titus bristles. "We were waiting on King Kael, and now that he's finally decided to grace us with his presence, I'll begin. Is that satisfactory, Henrick?" It's an obvious dig.

Henrick's steely silence causes tension to flare amongst the gathered men.

Ashton paces to a stop beside me, tilting his head to whisper in my ear, "Have you heard the rumors coming out of the packlands?"

"Not now," I murmur, throwing him a cautious look.

"Later, then. We'll see what this fool has to say for himself."

"What do you mean by that–"

Ashton paces away, coming to a stop near a crumbling column that twists all the way to the ceiling, and leans against it, crossing his arms over his chest.

"Queen Morgathra has offered us a deal," Titus begins, his clipped words echoing over the crackling lightning. "She'll release some of the hostages from our kingdoms if each of us gives her ten dragons each–trained warriors."

Ashton's sharp laugh cuts through his words. "What kind of trade is that? She has dragons. She has our people as slaves–"

"She has women," Titus barks, teeth bared. "Women from each of our kingdoms… except his, of course." He throws a hand in my direction, the motion meant to be dismissive.

"Then why the fuck am I here? Any deals you make her won't affect me in the slightest," I drawl, running my tongue along my lower teeth.

"We're the last of the Dragon kings, Kael," he snaps, his words coming out in a hiss. "Morgathra already has us by the balls. Our mines–"

"You mean," I sneer, taking a step in his direction, "she's tired of you, an old, wrinkly fool of a man, warming her bed. And now it's in your best interest to try to sell the support of the other kings in her favor. You won't find any support from my kingdom. Starfall and the Emerald Coast will remain as they always have–removed from any business that has to do with the witches and their queens. Do not call on me again." I whirl, stalking away from the sorry looking group of kings, but Titus chuckles low.

"Your territory is closest to the borders of Vaeloria, Hexeton, and Luna Hollow. Whatever she's planning affects you directly, I fear."

I stop short of the crumbling entrance to the castle and turn, giving him a sharp, annoyed look. "Then enlighten me, Titus. Enough with the games and riddles. What the hell is Morgathra up to now, besides plucking the scales off her dragon slaves to strengthen the magic in her coven?"

I glance at Ashton, arching a brow. He shakes his head, mouthing, *"I tried to tell you!"*

"Morgathra recently had a great success in Vaeloria, her first step in finally cracking Queen Maeve's iron grip of influence on that kingdom and Hexeton," Titus drawls, tucking his spindly fingers behind his back as he paces. "Twenty-one years ago, she was… very rudely left out of a party held in honor of the birth of the Alpha of Ebonclaw's first, and so far only, child."

I narrow my eyes at the old man. "And I should care about this why?"

"Because that baby was special," Titus murmurs, arching a silver eyebrow at me as he turns, directing his voice to Ashton and Henrick. "A baby that shouldn't have been possible, and the Alpha knew it. He made a deal with a witch from Morgathra's coven when his mate, his Luna, fell ill during her pregnancy. He went back on their terms, and when that child was born, Morgathra came to collect," he says with a hiss, smiling around the words like they're a tasty meal. "When the

Alpha refused to pay up, Morgathra cursed the child in front of the king and his court, telling him that if she stepped foot beyond the castle grounds before the moonrise of her twenty-first birthday, she'd fall into an eternal sleep. She told the king that his child would prick her finger on a rose's thorn–that beauty would be her demise. So, he kept the princess hidden away all these years and just a few nights ago… Morgathra's curse came to fruition."

A knot forms in my stomach, yanking tight against my spine. "Morgathra has no business with the wolf shifters of Vaeloria."

"But their allegiance to Queen Maeve of Hexeton is a threat," he snaps. "It's a threat to all of us. Morgathra means to invade, to start her war against Maeve, and she wants us to aid her, to stand behind her–"

"Her war?" I ask sharply, taking a step toward him. "Her war for–what? Being bested by a wolf who came to her aid in a time of need and didn't have the means to pay her coven? What was asked of him, I wonder? His Luna's life in exchange for the baby she was carrying? Or, her war for dominance over the mortal lands against the very witch who cast her out of Hexeton? I'm not getting in the middle of a witch's vendetta against another witch." My voice booms through the area, sending a rattle through the ancient stone. A few pebbles slide free from the crumbling columns. Ashton carefully edges away from the column he was leaning against, looking over his shoulder to ensure he isn't about to be buried alive.

"We will give Morgathra what she wants," Titus sneers.

"You're on your own," I tell him, my voice lowering to a rasping snarl.

I turn from the group, stalking out of the sanctum once used by the many kings and queens of the mountains that hug the northern edge of the continent. Dozens whittled down to four.

Once, this mountainous hellscape was called Drakthor. Now, there's barely anything left to give a name.

Footsteps follow me through the winding, stone-lined hallways. I take a sharp left toward the entrance I used when I arrived but pause, allowing the footfalls to catch up with me.

"Don't tell me you're considering joining forces with Morgathra," I say into the darkness.

Ashton chuckles wryly. "What kind of man do you think I am, Kael?" His voice simmers, however, when he adds, "But Morgathra does have several women held captive in her covens that belong to us–at least, Henrick and me."

"Then pledge your aid to Queen Maeve instead. Hell, pledge your loyalty to the kings and Alphas of Vaeloria, if you must. They have armies."

"So do you," he says quietly, his silver eyes shining bright despite the darkness swallowing us whole.

I grind my teeth. "You know what I protect. You're the only other dragon I've allowed into my territory. I'm not risking my people–"

"I'm losing my territory with each passing day," he says, his voice barely above a whisper. "Our kind is dying out with each passing year, Kael. I know your people thrive, but how many babies have been born? A few here and there? One or two a year? Every five to ten years, if you get lucky? Morgathra and her coven are to blame. Her dark magic has the mountains in a chokehold. You can't hide from that, even tucked away in the mist as you are. Queen Maeve won't involve herself unless Morgathra makes a move for Hexeton, and she's already sinking her teeth into Vaeloria, so they're on the precipice of damning everything to hell. Her magic will come for you, especially when she learns the dragon kings aren't going to bend to her will and aid her conquest. She's been building her coven against Queen Maeve for over a decade now."

"And what," I cut in sharply, "does a princess of Vaeloria have to do with any of this? A wolf shifter, no less."

He shrugs, his body no more than a shadow. "I don't know, but perhaps you should find out."

"Me?" I laugh as he steps past me. I follow him through the crumbling tunnel, stepping over ancient debris and rock. "Why?"

"Like you said, Kael. Why not throw your aid behind the shifters of Vaeloria and find out from the Alpha himself? He has an army, remember?"

The stormy sky opens up around us at the end of the tunnel, illuminating our bodies in sharp, blue shadows as lightning crackles overhead.

"Go to Ebonclaw and find out the truth before Titus can force us into a corner. Otherwise, I believe this might be it for our kind." Ashton turns to me, waving, before letting himself fall backward over a rocky ledge.

A few seconds later, a massive silver dragon parts the sky, barreling upward with his scaled wings tucked tight, and disappears into the clouds.

He's always been one for a dramatic exit, I'll give him that.

He's also, unfortunately, right.

If there's going to be a war... I need to get ahead of it, and that means making some deals with those soft-pawed dogs of Ebonclaw.

TO EBONCLAW

Kael

I ALREADY KNOW I'M DREAMING WHEN MY EYES CATCH ON RAYS OF milky sunlight. Soft, white curtains dance in a warm breeze scented with salt and ozone, like a storm is passing over the mountaintops. Shadows dance through the beams, the familiar, yet dreamlike, room all around me fading into temporary darkness as the heavy clouds drift in front of the sun, but the air is warm and inviting as I sit up, smoothing the satin duvet over my lap, and turn toward the piano.

I've had this dream enough times to know what I'm looking for and where to find it–to find her. Her thin fingers brush over the keys, plucking and grazing through each soft, echoing note of a song I know by heart but can never remember when I wake up.

Golden blonde hair tumbles down her back, vibrating with each faint, practiced movement of her wrists and fingers, her narrow shoulders loose as she sways with the music, playing like the notes are coming from a place deep within her–her heart–her very soul.

Sometimes I tell her to come back to bed. Sometimes I rise, my bare feet biting into the chilled stone floor inlaid with gems and crystals. Sometimes I make it to her before being pulled from the dream and run my hands down her bare arms, leaning down to breathe in her scent—roses. A garden in full bloom.

Another cloud passes over the sun and holds, and the room is enveloped in stormy darkness, like always.

But the dream doesn't dissolve. She keeps playing that song like she's stuck, unable to move. I slowly, carefully, ease off the mattress.

"Come to bed," I whisper, my voice hazy and distant. I reach for her, smoothing my hands down her arms like I always do. A glimmer of my scales, my powers, sparkle under my skin when I bring my hands up again, leaning down to brush a kiss to the top of her head.

She leans into my touch, sighing softly, but her fingers keep dancing over the keys.

We've never made it this far before. Maybe this is the moment I'll see her face. I've been waiting.

"You must find me, Kael." She breathes into the music. Her voice is both familiar and totally strange, bleeding into the soft song she keeps playing over, and over. "I'm waiting for you. I can feel you now."

She leans her head back against my abdomen, her face cast in shadow as she looks up into my eyes. My fingers drift along her jaw, under her chin, my thumb brushing over the curve of her lips, trying to map and memorize the face I can't see in the darkness.

She's a figment of my imagination. She doesn't exist in my reality. I know that for a fact. Because she's my *mate*, and the odds of a dragon finding their mate is so rare it's a legend—a fable. A dusty, forgotten myth.

But the dream continues in startling clarity. I lean down as she looks up, her neck bent to gaze into my face. I press my lips to hers and feel it—that pull. That yanking of the strings that bind us, singing the same song she plays nightly on her piano.

"Come to bed," I whisper against her mouth. "Stay with me." My hands travel over her shoulder and down the slope of her breasts. She inhales sharply, her lips parting over mine. "Stay with me," I repeat, but I feel the dream falling away, disintegrating all around me.

"Help me," she whispers, her voice strained as it fades. "You must find me. I'm waiting for you."

"What is your name?" I call out into the swelling darkness, but the dream shatters, falling away like mist as I'm sucked into darkness and spit out in the same room, in the same bed.

Rain streams down the windows full of frosted stained glass in shades of dark blues and greens. Beyond, just out of sight, a sprawling city rests in a valley below my castle built into the towering mountainside, cloaked by mist.

I run my hand over my face, then drag it down over my chest to rest against my thundering heart. My muscles are flexed and rigid like I'm on the verge of shifting. It takes several seconds to calm down enough to sit up, shaking sleep from my body while rubbing my fists against my eyes. I blink into the darkness hugging the room, my gaze resting on the corner where my dreams like to focus, but it's empty. There isn't, and hasn't ever been, a piano there.

I reach for the journal resting at my bedside, trying to conjure the details, but my pen hovers over the page–the first page, where only a few things are written. Her blonde hair–like liquid gold. Her rose scent. The soft, airy feel of her skin under my touch.

I tried, once, to remember the song enough to scratch down the notes but it's impossible. There's nothing to add but...

I write down what she said to me. Find me. I'm waiting for you. *Help me.*

My senses flare as I scribble those last two words.

I'm a dragon. I guard what's mine to the death. Even in my dreams, this woman belongs to me, and only me. The idea that this figment of my imagination is in danger... rattles me to my core. I have to remind myself she doesn't exist, that I'm making her up, like my subconscious is reminding me of my maturity, my ability to produce an heir, but... dragon babies are as rare as mates these days.

"Alpha," comes a deep male voice as I cross into my study sometime later, dressed and somewhat ready for the day. Ryker, the commander of my forces, walks into view, rubbing his hands together against the chill in the air before stepping behind me into my study. I close the door behind him, blinking blearily at the ground before raising my gaze to meet his.

He's tall, broad—a typical dragon male—but he's rough around the edges and heavily scarred, his dark brown hair falling around his face and shoulders as the muscles flex beneath his shirt.

"What did you find out?"

"We couldn't get into Vaeloria," he says, sucking his teeth and tucking his hands in the pockets of his pants.

"What do you mean you couldn't get in?" I sink into my desk chair, exhausted from another night spent lost in my dreams.

Ryker leans against the wall near one of the windows, pulling the curtains back to look outside, but we're high in the mountains, and there's nothing to see but thick, unending rain clouds. "There's a wall of warriors guarding the city. I've never seen anything like it. I sent Zaden ahead to try to talk to them, to tell them we were here to see the Alpha King of Ebonclaw, but they didn't respond. They held their ground."

I lean back, swiveling in my chair. "Held their ground?"

"None of them moved," he explains. "Some were in human form while others were in their wolf forms. But we were outnumbered, and I wasn't going to risk shifting and turning an entire city against us. You know how the witches and shifters feel about dragons."

I nod. "You made the right call." Chances are highly likely the majority of those in Vaeloria don't even believe we're real. It's been... decades since I set foot outside of Drakthor. Decades that have passed in a blink of an eye, it feels. Decades mean nothing to us. We're not immortal, so to speak, but our lives can stretch for centuries as long as we aren't killed by other dragons or lose our powers to the witches.

I rise, tapping my knuckles on the desk before saying, "I'll go myself."

He blows out a breath. "The shifters have the whole city surrounded," he argues.

"And for good reason. You've confirmed my suspicions just by laying eyes on their territory." I grab a piece of paper off the desk, searching for a pen while continuing, "I want as many guards patrolling the peaks as you can spare from regular patrol. Lock down the city and villages. No one goes into the sky in my absence unless they're under your command." I find a pen, scribbling a note. "I'll be back before sundown." I glance at the clock resting on the wall. "Twelve hours from now. In the meantime, have one of your flyers take this to Terminus. It's urgent."

Ryker nods obediently, plucking the note from my fingers and tucking it in his pocket.

The last thing I wanted to do today was go to Vaeloria to confirm Ashton's rumor of civil unrest in the kingdoms of magic, but here I am, walking up the spiral staircase leading to the very top of my mountaintop palace, a castle built into and within this sacred mountain millennia before my birth. Wind and rain whips across my face, rustling my inky-black curls as I shed my jacket, tossing it on the rain-soaked landing platform built atop the peak. I shake out my tired muscles in preparation, then close my eyes.

Instead of darkness, I see her. I see her fingers pulling across the keys of her piano. I hear that song again, calling out to me, begging me to remember.

Pressure erupts, edging on pain, before my body rolls and tears, changing from a mere man—flesh, and bone—to something greater.

The clouds part as jet-black scales cover my body. I shoot from the platform, my massive black wings expanding only once before I launch into the heavens...

To Vaeloria.

Because, for the first time in modern, written history... the dragons are aligning with the wolves.

The sky remains dark and stormy the entire two hour long flight. It's uneventful. The mountains bleed into rolling, barren plains, then that thick, unending forest creeps into my sight, spreading out for dozens upon dozens of miles until the first villages come into view, rushing past me as I coast just out of sight, a shadow sprinting through the clouds.

I land in silence, shifting into my human form before my feet even touch the ground. My scales become that suit of black armor glinting with gems, the same suit I'd been wearing when meeting with the dragon kings.

It's been four days since that meeting. Four nights spent in dreamland, trying to feel something other than the crushing weight of the evil coming for us—for me and my dwindling people.

I reach the clearing where Ryker and his two warrior dragons landed, their scents mingling with the soft spring grass and blooming flowers creeping from beneath the shadow of the trees.

Within minutes, I reach the border of Vaeloria, the midday sun casting a glare over the line of warriors standing in wait.

They don't make a sound. They don't move at all as I cautiously approach. My heart barely beats as my feet move over the grass and into the sparse trees that surround the stunning, sun-soaked city less than a mile away.

"My name," I call out, my voice booming, bouncing from tree to tree, "Is Kael of Starfall, Dragon King of the Emerald Coast. I'm here to call on the Alpha King of Ebonclaw!"

No movement. No murmured voices. Nothing.

I move closer. "I demand an audience with your king!"

A whisper of wind drifts through the group, rustling fur and clothing, but no one moves and…

I realize why.

Everyone is asleep, their eyes closed, their lips slightly parted as they rest standing straight up, like they fell into a dead kind of slumber with a second's notice.

THE CURSE

Kael

Vaeloria is lost to slumber. I can taste the magic on my tongue–a heady, metallic sheen I can't swallow down. Villagers slump against barrels and crates, snoozing peacefully, their bodies damp with the rain that passed through sometime yesterday.

Thank the old gods it's summer. They would have frozen solid last night otherwise.

Even the children lie in heaps of homespun fabric as I move through the outer villages. The shutters and doors of the humble cottages I pass on my way to the castle clap against their stone walls, left open, unlocked.

The air is still, and the silence is overwhelming, especially when I pass a group of chickens in the center of a dirt road, the entire flock asleep with their heads tucked under their wings.

Warriors slump against the wall surrounding the castle. The gate is open, creaking in the warm wind that rustles through the immaculate garden.

People dressed in finery spread out over the glistening, white stone steps leading to the grand entrance, like they left in a hurry but not quick enough to escape this... curse. This dark, creeping magic that has Ebonclaw in a chokehold. From the top of the stairs I have a view of the other small villages that hug Ebonclaw's castle. No smoke rises from chimneys. The sound of carriages bumping along the dirt roads doesn't carry through the breeze. In the distance, larger buildings rise above the forest in the sun's glare. Vaeloria is a large, sprawling city. There're dozens of Alphas and Lunas who claim this territory, as well as witches under Queen Maeve's leadership and a scattering of humans. I wonder if they've been affected by this magic yet, but that investigation will have to wait.

I push the grand doors open with a creak that echoes through the wide, ornate foyer. Servants, maids, and guests from what looks like a ball lie on the ground. I crouch to determine whether they're dead or merely sleeping. It's just sleep, but there's nothing I can do to wake them up.

I follow the trail of sleeping guests to the ballroom and pause in the doorway, my blood running cold as ice as I look up at the... the creeping vines and thick brambles crawling across the ceiling, across the floor, choking the ballroom in shades of brown and black. It stinks like filth, like death, as black flowers bloom and wither against the roping vines.

The vines are coming from the throne at the far end of the ballroom. A low moan ripples toward me over the breathily snores of the guests. I pick my way through the crowd of cursed party goers, up the short steps to the throne platform, and feel my breath catch in my throat.

The Alpha King of Ebonclaw is trapped in the vines, pinned to his throne.

I lengthen my talons, my fingers shifting into something dragon-like, and slice through the foliage until the vines fall away, sizzling before wilting to ash.

The king, he's... awake, gasping for breath as I pull him from the throne and lay him at my feet, kneeling to get a better look at him.

"Get out," he rasps, his throat dry and aching from lack of use. "Get out while you can."

"Who did this to you?"

He licks dry lips. His eyelids flutter. I can't tell if he's on the verge of death or falling into the same unending slumber as his people. "Morgathra."

"Why?"

"My daughter." He chokes, his eyes watering. He's a large man—portly, like he lives a life where he's only known comfort. His dark red hair and beard shimmer in the sunlight as he turns his dark brown eyes to mine. "Morgathra… she cursed her. She promised she would when I refused to give her up. I couldn't give her to that witch. She tricked me, all those years ago, when my Luna fell ill."

"Where is the princess?"

"I don't know," he breathes painfully, eyes watering. "Morgathra said that if Maxiana shed a single drop of blood before the moonrise of her twenty-first birthday, the curse would take hold. I kept her safe. I didn't let her leave the castle walls. Her whole life was—was guarded, and she was safe. She was supposed to—to come into her powers, and it would have broken the curse. I held a ball in her honor, meaning to bring her out to meet her pack for the first time once the sun had set, and the moon had risen but—"

He seizes, his eyes rolling back in his head.

"Alpha King?" I say firmly, shaking his shoulders.

But he slumps, letting out a breathy sigh, and falls asleep.

I lean down to listen to his mortal heart. A gentle thump, thump, thump greets me.

Annoyed and more than frustrated, I let him go and rise, looking around at the mess that witch left behind. The vines are growing in real time, and soon they'll take over the castle, then bleed out into the village. They curl and coil around the sleeping bodies scattered on the floor, but no one wakes up.

No one makes a sound.

What can I do?

What is there to do?

I start walking out of the ballroom, making a mental checklist. I'll send dragons to the village to gather the people back into their homes, to lock doors and keep them safe from the elements. It's a start, at least, until I can find a way to get a meeting with Queen Maeve, who has never trusted the dragons–and with good reason. But this curse… it's spreading.

I cross into the foyer as the vines coil across the marble floor, reaching toward the first of the guests in their path.

A scurrying of footsteps echoes toward me through the hallways branching off of the foyer. I whirl, my wings erupting before I can stop the transformation, but my human body remains intact.

A tattered woman runs into view before skidding to a stop with a scream at the sight of me. She tries to shy back into the shadows, but I rush for her, clasping her arm before she can escape.

"Who are you?" I sneer, yanking her back into the light. "Are you a witch?"

"N-No!" she cries out, terrified as her eyes scan my wings, then my glimmering black eyes. "I'm just a maid!"

"Why aren't you cursed like the rest?"

"I don't know," she blubbers, choking on the words. "I've–I've been trying to find help for my princess–she's–she won't wake up. No one will wake up. I've tried everything. Now, I can't get to her at all. The door is blocked."

I let her go, and she stumbles away from me, panting, her soft brown hair falling loose over her shoulders. She smells like a shifter. Her gray maid's uniform is filthy, torn in several places. Grime smudges her cheeks as her eyes fill with tears.

"What's your name, girl?"

"Annabel," she whimpers, sniffling. She wipes her nose on her sleeve, her eyes barely able to hold mine.

"What happened here?"

"Morgathra's curse came to fruition," she whispers, her face twisting with grief. "And Max was… She had no idea. She didn't know why she had to be kept away, locked in this castle, never left alone, even while she slept. She was so close to the moonrise, too."

"Where did Morgathra take her?"

Her eyes meet in the shadows. My wings tuck in tight, fading away. She seems to relax a little more when they're gone.

"Morgathra didn't take her," she replies. "She's–she's in the tower. I've been trying to get in for days now but the vines… they're taking over the entire castle."

"Show me."

She nods, her face flushing with hope I'm going to hate to see drain from her cheeks. The maid leads me through the castle to a door already covered in thick, twisting vines. I cut through them with my talons, but they grow back quickly despite my best efforts. I manage to get inside, cutting through vines as thick as my forearm as I climb the narrow, winding stone staircase. But the door at the top is… totally blocked. Vines thicker than my neck block the entrance completely. I tear at them, but it's no use.

"Fuck," I hiss, stepping away from the door as smaller, fresh vines try curling around my ankles.

I start to climb down when I hear… music. A twinkle of keys, like a music box is being wound, and the notes are playing in soft whispers, but… *I know that song.*

My body reacts before my mind has a chance to catch up. I know that song. I hear it in my dreams. I only remember it in my dreams.

There's no way the woman lying cursed in this tower is… my mate. She's a shifter–a wolf, not a dragon.

I'm losing my mind. My senses are off because of the curse all around me.

I tear myself away from the tower and reach the base of the stairs as the vines stretch toward me at an alarming rate.

Annabel is still there, trembling with nerves.

I grab her arm, deciding in the moment I can't leave her behind to die or fall victim to the curse. "Go find some clothes. Warm ones. The warmest clothing you have."

"What? Why?"

"You're not staying here."

"Where am I going?"

I swallow, trying to be as gentle as possible with the poor little wolf as her lower lip begins to tremble. "With me."

"But–"

"Coat. *Now.*"

She pales but turns, hurrying down the hallway, stepping over the vines. I follow, my nostrils flaring as I try to pick up any scents I might find familiar, but this place is entirely... wolf. The curse's stench cuts through those warm wolf undertones like rancid, festering blood.

Annabel turns into a room, and my body locks up tight.

Roses. It smells like roses here.

"Max won't mind," she says tearfully, fetching a thick, wool coat out of the closet.

I find it impossible to swallow past the knot in my throat when I scan the room and see the piano in the corner. I close my eyes. "Find pants, too. Socks and boots."

"But it's summer–"

"Do it," I growl, and the maid obeys, but she whimpers as she gathers the warmest clothes she can find and puts them on.

I walk to the piano and pluck one of the keys.

"She loves to play. It's her favorite thing," Annabel whispers across the room, the words laced through a sob.

There's nothing I can say to make this better for Annabel. There's nothing I can say, period, because my mind is tangled with hazy memories of my dreams. I reach for them, but they're still lost in my subconscious, the details hazy when I'm awake.

Annabel yelps, and I whirl. Vines snake into the bedroom, curling and twisting as they reach for us.

"Come on. We need to go."

"Go where?" she asks, but cries out when I pick her up. She's going to freeze regardless of the coat, thick wool-lined pants, and boots, but I have no other choice, and this woman... she knows the princess well, knows about the curse in detail, I surmise. I need her to unravel the mystery while I find a way to act.

I hurry her through the castle, carrying her as I dart over the vines now trying to stretch toward the ceiling. They trail down the steps into the garden as I run into open air and launch into the sky, my wings erupting first before my body twists into my dragon form.

Annabel screeches and immediately passes out from shock. I keep her tucked in my talons, guarding her body with my radiant warmth, and part the clouds as the vines lift from the towers, trying to catch us, but I'm faster than a witch's curse.

When I'm above the clouds, I send a message to Ryker through the link that binds my pack, sending the words directly into his mind, hundreds of miles away, my magic straining to get the job done. "Send dragons to Vaeloria. *Now.*"

SHE'S A WITCH

Maxiana

The world is hazy and dark as I move through water so shallow it barely brushes my ankles. It ripples with each step I take, disturbing the millions of stars reflected on its surface. It's totally dark here save for the stars hanging overhead, and silent, even as I splash through the water.

I have no idea how I got here, but I feel like I've been stuck in an endless, watery, starlit loop for hours now. My long, white slip of a dress floats on the surface, gathered around my ankles, as I move through the nothingness, wondering when it's going to end.

Soft, whispered voices drift around me—unfamiliar and tangled, like they're speaking underwater. I must be dreaming, right? There's no way this is real. This endless, shallow ocean of stars is a figment of my mind, my too-active imagination. It has to be.

I pause, squinting into the dizzying starlight. A small rise is just visible in the distance, I believe. An island cloaked in shadow and mist, but there is, in fact, land.

My chest convulses with relief as I pick up the pace, breaking into a run. But it feels like no matter how fast my feet carry me, the island is getting further away.

"Please!" I grind out, gathering my dress so it doesn't slow me down by dragging in the water. "Please!"

Mist begins to coil around my legs, blocking the light from the stars completely as it envelops me. I lose sight of the island, but then I'm stepping upward. The water falls away, and small, smooth pebbles bite into the bottoms of my feet.

I climb out of the mist, and then I'm...

I'm dreaming. This is, for sure, without a single doubt, a dream.

The pebbles beneath my toes aren't rocks, no. Glimmering gems spread out across a wide shoreline, flickering like they're lit from within with the same starlight overhead. In fact, I'm closer to the stars now. I reach up, plucking one with my hand, curling my fingers around it. I look down at the... the star in the palm of my hand. It's golden, shimmering, and warm to the touch.

"We mine them," a deep, rumbling male voice says nearby. "They fall from the sky and settle in the mountains. It takes a while and a lot of work to find them, but they're sacred to us."

I turn to the voice. A tall, broad figure stands only a few yards away, his body cloaked in shadow. But his eyes... I can see them—see the stars reflected in them, at least.

"This isn't real," I whisper, more to myself than to him, but his soft, deep chuckle reverberates through my body, and it feels... very real, indeed.

"I question it all the time. Every night. Every time I close my eyes." I watch as he crouches to dig his fingers into the shoreline, gems falling between them as he scoops them up and turns to me. "Come here."

My feet carry me to his side on their own accord. But even so close to him now, I can't see his face. He's just... a shadow. I wonder if he can see me at all, or if I'm just a slice of darkness in his eyes, too.

He hands me several games—emeralds, rubies, and sapphires. They're perfectly smooth and round, heavy despite their small size.

"Where are we?" I ask, my voice like a lullaby drifting in the still, night air.

"I'm not sure, but you called me here," he says under his breath as he places another gem in my hand, his fingertips grazing the underside of my fingers. I curl them around his on impulse, like we know each other, the touch bordering on intimate.

"I… who are you?"

"Tell me your name, and I'll tell you mine," he says.

My mouth opens, lips parted to whisper my name into existence, but nothing comes out. It's like… I've forgotten it. I can't remember my own name.

"I don't know it," I admit, looking into his star-flecked eyes.

"I've forgotten mine, too."

"How is that possible?"

"Because we're dreaming," he whispers, and I feel his touch on my cheek, his thumb brushing over my cheekbone. He's familiar. Something about his touch sends prickles of warmth skittering over my chilled skin, warming me in places no one has ever seen or touched. But he knows me, and I know him… the man from my dreams.

This is the closest we've ever been.

"Stay with me," he whispers against my skin, his lips grazing my cheekbone. "Don't leave yet. Stay here with me."

I grip his wrist, squinting into the darkness to try to see him, but I can't. He's a shadow, a ghost, just a feeling of warmth with a solid body, but… his details are lost to the darkness.

"Stay with me," he repeats, his voice low as we kneels, our knees touching.

"How do I find you outside of my dreams?" I ask, but his lips… touch mine. A soft but tender pressure that makes me inhale sharply in anticipation for more.

"I'll find you. I promise," he replies before his mouth closes around mine, and… it doesn't feel like a dream. This feels very real.

I gasp around his mouth when his tongue slides over my lower lip, then dips inside, exploring. It slips around mine in a dizzying, heated, but slow, dance while he groans.

The gems slide from my hands. I reach for him, finding him in the darkness, and grip his sides, finding just… skin.

And then I realize my dress is gone. It's a dream, after all. His hands travel down my arms to my thighs, warm, large, and solid against my skin. Ripples of gooseflesh erupt under his heated touch, and I'm lost to him the second he pulls me into his lap, whispering against the ridge of my ear, "Stay with me. Just a little longer."

I close my eyes as he presses a hungry kiss to my jawline then down my neck. He grips my sides, lifting my breasts to his mouth, where he feasts, licking and sucking my skin with a fierce intensity that makes my nipples peak, hardening under his touch.

"Stay," he practically begs, growling the word against my skin.

I lock my legs around his waist, my lips parted in a heady moan against his temple when one of his hands dips down toward the apex of my thighs.

He rocks against me, straining as he groans, his fingers gliding down, parting my folds and I'm… I'm…

"My mate," his hisses through gritted teeth. "You belong to me. Always."

He lays me down against the cool, smooth gems, his hands never leaving my body, like we're anchoring each other to this realm, this dreamland. He splays my legs apart as he lowers himself between them, whispering praise over my cheeks, down my neck, my chest, my breasts… where his teeth graze my nipples, and lower, whispering, "Mine. I've been waiting for you my entire life. You are mine."

"I'm yours," I echo, caressing his face. He's blocking the starlight, that's the only way I can tell he's hovering over me, face to face. His lips brush mine in a featherlight touch, like he's holding back, before he growls and kisses me like his life depends on it, and I feel pressure between my thighs.

I gasp as his thick, rock-hard cock nudges inside me. It doesn't hurt, though, not like I've heard it would the first time. Maybe because this is all just a wicked, delicious dream, but I digress. I lift my hips to meet his as he buries his cock so deep the stars overhead seem to burn brighter, flickering in time with my heartbeat.

My inner walls clench, vibrating around him, and he feels... amazing. He fills me up, stretching me out, every movement he makes causing my body to melt with want and desire that burns so deep I feel it building in my belly and thighs before he even begins to move again.

His hand drifts up my body to clutch my neck as he rises above me, rolling his hips against mine in deep, deliberate thrusts.

He's not gentle. He's not going easy on me in the slightest, and I thank the Goddess for it because I've waiting for him–for this–for so long, waking from these lustful dreams to my thighs slick with want, with a pressure I can't shake until I slide my own fingers through my wetness, imaging it's his hand there driving me to the point of insanity.

I don't dare close my eyes again lest the darkness swells, and I'm pulled from the dream before I'm ready, which I doubt I'll ever be.

He grunts loudly, driving into me so hard it forces a breath from my lungs, my scream of pleasure splitting through the stars all around us.

"Yes," he breathes. "Gods, yes, come for me, my angel." He presses me into the gems, rolling his cock into me so deep I might be hallucinating his strength and the way... that way his shadowed body lengthens into what I can describe as wings that block the starlight, casting me in his shadow.

A single tear trickles down the side of my face as he bares down into my body with one final, aching thrust, but... something clutches my ankles, squeezing and snaking upward over my calves.

It hurts. My bones scrape together. I cry out as I'm pulled from him.

"No, no, no!" he shouts, but his voice is suddenly distant as the dream shatters, turning to pure, violent darkness that... that hurts. It's so painful.

The snaking, coiling pressure wraps up my legs, pinching my hips as it drags me away from him, my body sliding over the gems until I feel water all around me again, but this time, it drags me under.

❦

KAEL

I WAKE WITH A START, DRENCHED IN SWEAT, MY BODY ACHING FOR release, but I'm struggling to breathe as I sit up, running my fingers through my hair, damp with sweat.

I still feel like she's beneath me, writhing and moaning, her hands gripping my hips until her nails bite into my skin. She felt so... so good. So tight, so perfect.

And then the vines...

I roll out of bed as thunder booms and lightning crackles, illuminating my bedroom in ropes of electric blue that split the sky into pieces. Rain streams down the windows while I hastily dress. It's the middle of the night. My heart thunders, damn near bursting out of my chest when I rush through the doorway of my room and into the spiderweb of hallways of my castle deep within the mountain's peak.

I must have woken up on instinct, my senses aware that the dragons I sent to Vaeloria to deal with the villagers outside of the cursed castle have returned.

I storm into the wide, cavernous space with a winding stone staircase leading to the very top of the peak where my dragon warriors just landed.

Ryker is the first to appear, coming down the stairs in his scaled, glimmering black armor, soaking wet. His eyes are weary and tired when he spots me, shaking his head. "What the fuck happened there?"

"How bad is it now?"

"Vines everywhere. We could barely reach the village. We got some people inside, but it's useless. The vines got a hold of one of the warriors, but we freed him just in time. They stretched from every building, every tower, when we flew away."

I run my fingers through my hair. "And the tower in the castle? Were you able to breach it?"

"The castle is... overrun by vines. It's like a forest, Kael. The vines are as thick as trees and coated in thorns. We couldn't even get through the gate."

I'm thrust back into my dream for a split second. The details are already fading, but I try as hard as I can to remember everything, especially her voice, the feeling of pressing my lips against her soft skin.

She'd been cloaked in shadow so thick I couldn't see her face, but she was… perfect. Everything. She is my mate, I know that for a fact now.

But the *vines* came for her, which confirmed something I'm still not entirely understanding.

"The royal maid I brought back with me," I begin as several warriors in their human forms, just as sopping wet as Ryker, funnel down the stairs, "She needs to start talking. I want you to get her to do that, by whatever means possible."

"Where is she now?"

"Sleeping off the journey here. She's in the infirmary. Warm her up for me, Commander. Make it clear I'm not fucking around. She knew about the curse on the princess. I need to know how to break it."

THE PRISONER

Kael

RAW GEMS MAKE THE OBSIDIAN WALLS GLITTER ALL AROUND THE MEEK,
pale, mentally exhausted young woman loosely chained to a bed in
the normally empty infirmary. A dragon shifter–a female–in a tidy
black uniform and creamy white cloak moves around her, swiping
another layer of thick, scentless salve made of crushed diamonds on
Annabel's arms and legs, healing the injuries she sustained in battle
against the vines.

I hadn't noticed her injuries before. Not her hands, which were so
raw they're now bright red as fresh, new skin develops. Not the lacer-
ations and blisters along her calves that are healing in real time.

She'd fought, but for what? Her own life? The life of her princess,
which she hasn't said a word about in the hour she's spent in Ryker's
company? That's what he just told me in the hallway, his normally
stern, unfazed disposition wore thin, like he'd just been through
battle.

I pull up a chair beside the bed and stare at the girl who refuses to meet my eyes. Ryker leans in the doorway, tsking his tongue at the healer in a command to leave, and she does, her white cloak billowing out behind her. Ryker leans on the door to close it, and Annabel flinches at the sound of the lock clicking into place but doesn't look at me. Her eyes follow Ryker's progress across the room where he positions himself against a wall with a full, head-on view of her and crosses his arms.

"How do you feel?" I ask.

She shimmies in the bed, rattling the lightweight chains keeping her bound to the room, at least for now. "Better." She glances at me wearily, crossing her arms around her stomach. She's wearing a cream-colored dress, and she's had the chance to bathe. She's a lovely woman for a shifter, I'll give her that. One glance at my terrifying second-in-command tells me he's noticed her quiet beauty. She's glaring at him, however. "I'd be totally fine if your beast hadn't chained me to the bed."

"It's to keep you safe," Ryker replies dryly, giving her a smug smile that lifts one side of his mouth.

"Safe from what? Dragons? I'm surrounded by them currently. I'm not sure how it could get any worse."

"You have a mouth on you for a shifter," Ryker growls, but Annabel rustles her chains, baring her teeth at him in response.

"You told my commander you were aware of the curse but refused to tell him why, or how you came into employment in the Alpha King of Ebonclaw's castle. I need to know about the curse in detail. It's spreading through Vaeloria, and I've just received word that Queen Maeve has shut down Hexeton, putting up wards against the curse to keep it away from her people–"

"She won't be able to stop it," Annabel whispers under her breath.

"Why not?"

Ryker shifters from foot to foot like he's uncomfortable under the weight of her words, her tone.

"It's a blood curse," Annabel explains, swallowing the words like they're painful. "The most powerful kind of magic there is. It'll spread like a disease until–until the next full moon, three weeks from now. If the curse isn't broken by then, it'll kill everyone under its hold, destroying Vaeloria and whatever villages it finds over the weeks."

"It's spreading fast. It will take Hexeton, possibly the human lands," I say, but Ryker's sharp intake of breath nearby makes me realize…. "And here, if it crosses into the mountains."

"How do we stop it?" he asks.

She shimmies on the bed again, her chains rustling and clinking together as she wrings her hands. "It's just a rumor. I don't know if it's true–"

"You need to tell us everything you know," I cut in sharply, losing my patience. "You seem keen on the princess. Do you want her to die?"

"No, she's my friend, but I failed her–"

"We will help you if you help us," Ryker growls, and she looks up at him, teary-eyed and flushed.

"You won't kill me after I tell you what I know?"

"Why would we?" I ask, genuinely curious how she came to that conclusion. The chains are one thing, and they are, in fact, for her safety. It would be entirely too easy for her to leave this room in a rush, looking for an exit, not realizing every exit from this mountain top fortress is a drop to the death for anyone without wings. She'd plunge to her death without realizing it before forever disappearing into the mist.

"Because Dragons hate witches," she whispers, narrowing her eyes and looking at Ryker through her lashes, somehow more afraid of him than she is of me. "And I'm not just a shifter, it turns out."

Ryker licks his lips. A strange expression passes over his rough, scarred features as he stares at Annabel, taking her in in a… strangely intimate way.

I lean back in my chair. "You're a hybrid?"

"Yes. My mother was a witch," she breathes, "and my father was some rogue shifter passing through her village, so the story goes. I was raised with the witches but cast out after my twenty-first birthday because I suddenly had the ability to shift. My mother had no choice but to take me to Vaeloria where someone like me would be accepted, someone *other*, someone *different*. I found employment at the Alpha King's castle and was tasked with… following the princess around, constantly. She was a teenager then. That was four years ago."

"Your powers–" I begin, but she cuts me off.

"I'm a healer, first and foremost. I have no gifts of light or nature, if that's what you're asking. I can't make it rain, make flowers bloom, or shoot light from my fingertips, but I have a knack for alchemy. I trained in apothecary medicine. And… the king began to trust me when I started healing the ailments of his staff. He told me about the curse when I asked why the princess wasn't allowed to go outside or to the village and why anything sharp had to be kept away from her." She looks down at her hands. "I slipped away for one moment, and it killed her."

"She's not dead yet, though, not until the full moon, right?" Ryker asks.

"I assume not," she replies with a tremble lacing through the words. "Blood magic is a… dark thing. It takes a lot of power to create a curse like this. Morgathra would have been… totally spent for years after casting the curse."

"That makes sense," I say, more to myself than to anyone in the room. "She wasn't seen or heard from for over a decade."

"Yes," Annabel confirms. "It would have taken her life force or parts of it. She's tied to the curse, just like Maxiana. They're both bound to it–giver and receiver. If Maxiana lives, if the curse is broken, it will kill Morgathra. If Maxiana dies, and the curse is about to reach its peak… I don't know, but I assume Morgathra will absorb the curse's strength and be more powerful than before."

She's dancing around what we really need to know, I can tell. Her eyes are downcast on her lap as she debates her next words.

I glance at Ryker, meeting his eyes. He steps forward, clearing his throat as he braces his large, scarred hands on the end of her bed. She pulls her legs up away from him, casting him a weary look. "How can we break a blood curse?"

She swallows hard, the column of her throat bobbing. "It's silly, but… true love's first kiss will break the curse."

Ryker chuckles darkly. "That's ridiculous."

"It's magic," she says. "Love is the most powerful magic of all, more powerful than a blood curse. The Alpha King was sure she'd find her mate on her birthday, during the ball. She'd also been so sure of it, but… I couldn't get back to her soon enough. I'm the reason this is happening."

"You're not," I tell her as gently as I can.

"It was my duty to protect her."

"By true love, do you mean her mate?" Ryker asks, still bracing his hands on the bed.

She looks up at him and holds his gaze for the first time. "Yes. That's the only way it'll work, but the vines are taking over the castle. They're impossible to destroy. The entire castle is probably overrun."

"I was able to get through some of them," I tell her, but she shakes her head.

"She's trapped in the tower. I don't know of any magic that could help free her at this point. Even if we found her mate by some miracle, it would be pointless. He wouldn't be able to access her."

"Well," Ryker breathes, "it's a good thing… the dragons are helping you, isn't it?"

She stares at him, teetering between glaring and nodding, it seems.

I rise from the chair and move toward the door. "That's enough for now. I have what I need. Ryker, see her into her own suite—something nice. Have her fed."

"Fed to what?" Annabel gasps before clamping her trembling lips closed again.

"We're not going to eat you," I snarl. "But you need food to survive, don't you? You're safe here. We'll remove the chains as long as you don't go exploring alone. Any exits to the castle are made for dragon shifters because we can fly, and you can't. You'll fall to your death."

She bristles, but I'm already turning to the door. My footsteps carry through the hallway, echoing as I enter the cavernous foyer and take the stairs to my study.

Half an hour later, Ryker joins me in the study, looking worn and uneasy as he slumps into a chair by the window. "How much time do you think we have to solve this before the curse spreads here?"

I flip through my ledger, tapping a pen on its surface while dropping into thought. "Two weeks, based on what you said the village looked like after I sent you back to take care of the villagers. We have some time, but not enough to locate her mate. That's impossible." I close my eyes against the sudden image of the woman from my dreams. Now, that's impossible. The princess can't be the same woman I've been dreaming about for the past year, but... the vines coming for her in the last dream do make me wonder if I'm looking at this all wrong.

"What do we do, Kael?" he asks, looking out the window.

"I don't know." It's an honest answer. "I'm going to Terminus to talk to Ashton, to warn him." I don't say that I'm thinking about dropping in and paying King Titus a visit, but... he's part of this if he's siding with Morgathra. I need to know what she promised him and what he offered her in return.

Ryker drops into silence for several seconds before saying, "Annabel has an odd scent."

"What?"

"You didn't catch it? She smells like rain." He continues absently looking out the window.

I lower my pen. I've never seen my commander like this, so lost in his own mind. He's normally sharp and constantly on edge, ready for battle in any given circumstance, but now?

"What's wrong with you?"

"Tired," he says, rising, dusting himself off. "I'll check on the witch before retiring. If you need me to come to Terminus with you, just say so."

"Stay here with Annabel. Make sure she has what she needs to be comfortable."

The mention of her name seems to send a shiver down his spine. I narrow my eyes at him as he slips from the room, closing the door behind him without so much as looking at me, his king, his oldest friend.

Something strange is afoot. Something that might undo the fabric of our world.

Maybe that's a good thing, for all dragons.

THE PRINCESS IS SOMETHING DIFFERENT

Kael

Terminus is always cloaked in storms. The raging, jagged mountain peaks shine white with every burst of lightning as I soar into Ashton's territory, parting the angry clouds and sending thick mist coiling around my dragon body as I tuck in my wings and spiral down into the shadowed valley of his territory.

Ashton's expecting me, which means I'm not bombarded by his guards as I glide onto a landing platform and slide to a stop near a set of massive iron doors guarding the mouth of his fortress.

Unlike Starfall, the largest city in my territory of the Emerald Coast, Terminus is built entirely within the mountains under Ashton's rule. Tunnels pass between the mountains, connecting his cities while protecting his people from the unforgiving elements. I shake ice from my wings before shifting back to my human form, breathing deeply past the stretch and pull of the transformation to fill my lungs with crisp, frigid air.

The massive doors open, and Ashton steps out, flanked by guards dressed in the kingdom's official uniforms of silver.

"You're an hour late," Ashton quips as I walk to him, clasping his hand in greeting. "Dinner's getting cold." His mouth pulls into a teasing smirk.

"I've never known you to greet anyone so warmly. I was expecting to hold this meeting outside, in the ice."

"Normally we would, but there's a storm coming this way within the hour. You're going to have to stay the night, I'm afraid. Come. I do have food on the table. Wine?"

"Do you have anything stronger?"

He chuckles, waving me into the shadowed recesses of his palace. The walls glimmer with polished obsidian and quartz as our footfalls echo from wall to wall. I've been here once or twice, but never for long. Being of similar age to Ashton has its benefits, like being allies, but also friends.

Still, he's a dragon. A dragon king, no less. He's secretive, especially about his people, his kingdom, and… his family.

A beautiful woman rises from a long, ornate table in the center of a wide, cavernous dining hall, her dark silver gown trailing down her elegant, slim body as she curtsies, her long white hair shimmering in the glow of the crystal chandelier hanging over the table.

"King Kael," she says gracefully, raising her head and meeting my eyes. Hers are a milky silver—a family trait, I suppose. I can already tell what color her dragon will be just by the look of her.

Ashton notices my shock and says kindly to the woman, "My dear, you've had a long day. Retire to our rooms for a while. I'll come check on you shortly."

She gives us both another graceful curtsy before turning and drifting away, her body passing through a darkened archway.

She's tall, but so are all dragon females… the rarest kind of the dragons of all. Women.

I turn to Ashton, who wearily looks after her, chewing his lower lip, before he motions for me to sit.

"I didn't realize you'd married," I say, sinking into a chair.

He grunts in response, pouring wine from a crystal pitcher into a matching glass, handing it to me. "A few years ago, yes. Her name is Elloura."

"She's a pearlescent dragon," I add. "I thought they went extinct."

He purses his lips as he sits opposite me, resting his elbows on the table, which is laden with food–roast meats of a wide variety, mostly. Piles of vegetables and fruit rest in bowls, while meat pies and small cakes tower in crystalline displays. It's a feast meant for a king. Two kings, I suppose.

"She's the last one." He sips his wine, looking slightly forlorn. I know better than to ask a dragon about his mate–whether fated or by marriage, but I had no idea Ashton had a queen, and I think there was a reason for that which goes beyond the rarity of her dragon form.

"I won't tell anyone about her existence."

"Thank you," he says, meeting my eyes. "She means more to me than I can possibly convey, and the last person I want sniffing around in our business is King Titus. And, he would, if he knew about her."

"Does she have the powers her people once possessed?"

"She can't control the weather, no. She's… Elloura is…" he struggles, and I notice the fine lines of fatigue on his normally fresh, young face. "She's weak, I'm afraid. She's been sickly since she was a child, from what she's told me. She was brought to my territory many years ago and was raised in one of the villages, but she came to serve in my court five years ago. I fell in love, Kael, if that's what you want to know."

"Is she your mate?"

"Close enough to it." He shimmies in his chair, glancing at the archway again. Then, he leans in, eyes holding mine. "We have…we have a child on the way, which is why I allowed this meeting to happen in the first place. You truly believe there's a threat against the dragons… I have to do what I can to ensure her safety, and the safety of our child, if it survives."

My stomach pitches. Normally, this kind of announcement would be a joyous occasion. Festivals are held in Starfall whenever a pregnancy is announced, but I know full well there's not much to celebrate until the baby is born safe into its mother's arms. With female dragons so scarce, losing one to childbirth is a tragedy felt across the kingdom. Losing both the mother and child is, unfortunately, a lot more common than the festivals held in their honor.

It's been happening like this for centuries now. Dragons don't procreate as often as the shifters and witches anyway with our long lives, but over the past decades, female dragons have become targets, shot from the skies they used to fly freely in.

The witches–Morgathra's coven, in particular–are to blame. Our scales and bones are used in their potions. They steal our power from the scales to strengthen their own. Our hearts are used to maintain their youth and for other nefarious reasons I've yet to figure out.

"No one will know about them," I assure Ashton, who exhales deeply, nodding despite the worry behind his eyes.

"It won't matter if what you say is happening in Vaeloria is true."

"Do you have reason to doubt me?"

He leans back, crossing his arms over his chest. "No."

"Then take my word for what it is–a promise that I'm doing what I can to ensure the dragon kingdoms remain safe from Morgathra's curse. I know you've sent your own scouts to the border to see the situation with their own eyes. Henry's forces, as well, but he's choosing to remain neutral. Blind to what's coming his way."

"Because the curse will spread to your territory first," Ashton quips. Then Henry's, then Titus's, then… Terminus.

"We have to act before it spreads to the base of the mountains north of Vaeloria."

He shakes his head. "Any interference that takes place in the magical lands to the south will be seen as an act of war against Queen Maeve. She has just a tight of grip on Vaeloria as she does Hexeton–"

"She abandoned Vaeloria and its people to the curse, choosing to ward Hexeton alone. It won't be enough to stop the curse's spread, but by the time she realizes that, it'll be too late for us, in the mountains."

"How long do we have?"

"It's a blood curse. We have a few weeks, at that, until the next full moon. If the curse isn't broken by then, there's nothing we can do."

"And how do you suppose we break a blood curse?" he asks sarcastically, chuckling. "They're unbreakable."

"This one has a loophole," I explain, holding my hands out in surrender. When he arches a brow, I explain how the shifter I rescued from the village, the only person who hadn't fallen under the curse, for whatever reason, turned out to be a witch who was given full knowledge about the curse that befell the princess.

Ashton's bright, cutting laugh splits the air in the dining hall. "True love's first kiss? Kael, be serious."

"I know–"

"True love as in this wolf princess's mate? What are we supposed to do, find him? The chances that he's part of her own pack are high, aren't they? He'd be cursed already. What are we going to do then? Carry him up to her tower and smash their faces together until they wake up?"

"Could there–" I begin, then cut myself off. My dreams haunt me in startling detail these days, little details forgotten when I'd first awoken now lingering in full color. Her soft skin. Her golden hair. Her scent of roses–the same as in the princess's rooms… and the vines. I blink, then hold Ashton's gaze. "Is there a chance a wolf shifter could be mated to something like us?"

"A wolf and a dragon?"

"Yes."

"What are you saying?"

"What if her mate isn't a wolf?"

"I suppose witches and wolves can be mates–"

"But what about dragons? Can we be mates with anything other than our own kind?" My voice carries around the room over the crackling fire directly behind Ashton, who's looking at me in stunned silence.

"No, of course not."

"You're sure?"

"I've never heard of it happening. Never read about it. Never heard whispers of it in the old tales of our kind."

"There was a time when our kind intermingled with the magical lands to the south, however. It could have very well happened–inter-breeding. Unions outside of dragons, shifters, and witches."

"You're talking about hybrids?" he scoffs, but I stand, unable to sit still any longer.

There was something I missed, something said before I knew anything about the curse that went over my head and fizzled into obscurity.

"Titus told us the princess of Ebonclaw was special," I murmur, clutching the top of my chair. "What did he mean?"

"Fuck if I know. I'm half convinced that man is in his last years–senile–" he begins.

"She's a hybrid," I grumble to myself, cursing my own stupidity for overlooking this detail. "She's not just a wolf; she's something else, something Morgathra thought was a threat."

"And? The vines have her trapped in that tower. According to you, she's in a dead sleep. And, we can't rope Titus into this without him running to Morgathra."

"I need... I need the full force of your army, your support."

He arches his brow again, sighing into his wine. "What are you suggesting we do?"

"We're going to get the princess out of her tower."

"How?"

I look down at my nails, letting my fingers transform into jet black talons with claws made of pure onyx.

"The chairs are antiques," Ashton sighs with a wince as my claws clutch the ancient wood.

"We cut through the vines."

"Impossible. My scouts already tried. They couldn't even get past the wall surrounding the village."

"Then we... take the entire tower."

"That castle is one of the oldest structures in both Vaeloria and Hexeton. Say we do that, tear the tower clean from its base, then what? It'll crumble within minutes, and the princess will fall to her death or be crushed by stone."

"We have to get her out of there if we're going to save our people," I tell him. "Will you fight for me, with me?"

"And what about Titus?" he asks under his breath. "What about King Henry?"

"King Henry will side with us when he realizes what's coming for him and his meager territory. Leave King Titus to me."

VISIONS OF THE PAST

MAXIANA

I'M ON THE BEACH AGAIN, THAT BEACH OF GEMS AND CALM, DARK water. Black mist hangs all around me as I walk in no single direction, unsure if I'm going to step off the beach and into a vat of inky, black nothingness again.

He's not here this time. I'm not sure how I know, but I can just… feel that I'm alone. Horribly, inexplicably alone.

I've never been alone. Never. Not a single day in my life.

I hug my arms to my chest as I pick across the beach. The mist begins to part, and through the starlight reflecting on the gems, I think I see the glow of a… a lantern. Yes, that flickering, soft amber light is stationary compared to the rippling glow of the stars shining against the gems.

The mist parts further, revealing a small, stone building with a single sconce lit on its side, right beside a door.

My heart rate skyrockets. I stumble over the gems in my haste to run, but I'm moving in slow motion, my movements dreamlike and hazy as I try to force my body forward over the beach. "Please!" I whisper breathlessly, reaching for the building, my fingertips straining as it grows closer and closer with each slow step. My entire body aches as I stretch my arm straight out, tears of pain plucking against my lashes before they fall, then lift off my cheeks, suspended like glimmering diamonds in thin air.

This has to be the exit of this dreamworld. This has to be the answer I've been searching for. A way out. I don't know how long I've been stuck here, but I have a ball to attend. I've been waiting for someone to wake me up, but no one has come for me.

I can't miss my own party. It's supposed to be the most important night of my life, the night I meet the man who visited me on this beach just… moments ago, right?

My fingers catch on the knob, curling and yanking in pure determination. The door gives way with an explosive blast of light.

The gem-lined beach falls away as I career into… bright, unforgiving sunlight. I shield my eyes but feel an overwhelming sense of dread that I've woken up. Like it's morning, and I slept through my birthday party, but then a soft twinkling of piano keys catches my attention–the same song I've played so many times, the song with no end, and no concrete beginning.

I lower my arm and blink into daylight streaming through crude windows lined with twisting alder branches. Sunlight fans through curtains covered in moth holes, and the room is made of… mud. Dried, hard mud and hay.

I whirl toward the piano music and find a young woman resting on the edge of the bed, humming as she knits what I think is a sock. There's no piano in sight, just her voice, soft, sweet, and lifted.

"Hello?" I gasp, my voice trembling. "Where am I?"

She continues humming without even looking in my direction. She's young–ay age, perhaps. Her hair is… long, and woven into a thick braid down her back that trails onto her hay stuffed mattress. Her hair is the color of liquid gold… just like mine.

"Hello?" I repeat, stepping toward her, but she doesn't look at me. She doesn't move when I try to lay a hand on her shoulder. My hand just… falls through her.

I pull my hand back with a yelp.

I'm still dreaming.

I'm still dreaming.

The young woman opens her eyes and stops humming abruptly. Her eyes are as blue as polished sapphires and… match mine exactly, down to the gold lashes.

This is my mother. I have no doubt about it.

"Mother?"

The young woman rises in alarm as the door to her room, which I realize is nothing more than a hut, opens, pouring sunlight across the dirt floor.

"Thisbe," an older woman with the same golden hair, streaked with pure white, says. "*Hide.*"

"Mama–"

"Now! Under the bed!"

Thisbe, my mother, panics as the woman, my grandmother, I assume, rushes toward her, tugging on her thin body toward the corner of the room. She turns to the bed, shoving it as hard as she can, but it barely moves. My mother jumps to help her, and the two of them move the bed, revealing a trap door.

"Get inside, now. Hurry!"

"What about you?" Thisbe cries, her eyes wet with tears. "Mama, please–"

My grandmother throws the trapdoor open revealing nothing but swelling, earthen darkness. "Go, Thisbe, my angel. Walk until you find the entrance to the old tunnels. They'll take you to Vaeloria. If you see anyone, or hear anyone, ignore it. They're not real. Don't listen to a word they say, I beg you." She pulls on Thisbe's thin, homespun dress as screams erupt from beyond the earthen hut. Screams of terror, then pain. Screams of such despair I feel my heart scattering as I watch my grandmother hug my mother–the kind of hug given when it's likely you'll never see that person again.

"Mama, please, come with me!"

More screams tear the air into shreds, closer this time. Snarls and growls explode, cutting through the screams of pain so immense I feel it in my bones.

But my grandmother shakes her head, tears flowing down her cheeks. "Go, my love. Don't let them find you." With a shove, my grandmother pushes my mother through the trap door, and closes it, pulling the bed back in place.

I blink, and the sunlight cuts out. It's silent save for the heavy, labored breaths of the woman beside me. I can only make out her eyes as she looks up at the holes in the trapdoor–little scraps of light dancing through sapphire hued irises. Fear I've never witnessed lingers there, especially as the screaming stops abruptly, and heavy footfalls echo from above.

"Where is she?" a male voice booms.

My grandmother doesn't answer, but her scream of pain soars through the air. Thisbe clamps her hand over her mouth to stop from crying out, choking on sobs as she backs into the darkness. More screams follow before shuddering out, but my mother keeps moving, step after step, sob after silent sob, until darkness consumes her.

I can feel her next to me as she turns and begins to feel along the walls. Snarling and growling echo behind us. Smoke begins to creep toward us, like her village is being burned to the ground, burying my mother alive.

I reach out, trying to touch her, but she's just a figment of my imagination–my dream.

My vision of the past.

I never knew her. The stories I was told were from her time as Luna of my pack. My father told me the moment he laid eyes on her, he fell in love. She was his mate, but he never went into detail about how, and when, they met.

Or where she'd come from.

All I knew is that she was a rare kind of wolf–with golden fur, pure, unblemished gold. No one had a coat like hers.

Thisbe's sobs go from silent to choked the further we move through the tunnel. Eventually our silent footsteps meet stone, and the dirt walls turn to stone, but it's still completely, utterly dark.

She passes several entrances to other tunnels, murmuring to herself through sobs. She has no idea how to get out of here, which direction to take, so she keeps moving forward, her legs trembling as the tunnel stretches on, and on, with no end in sight.

She hums her song, the notes carrying her pain and despair. When we reach a fork, however, she pauses, choking for breath, and rests her hands on her knees.

"Goddess help me," she whispers, sniffling. "Take my mother into Your loving embrace. Carry her to the stars to illuminate my path." She sniffles again, whimpering as she continues, "Mama. Oh, Mama! Wh-what do I do?"

I go to lay my hand on her back and… touch her.

She screams, flinching away from my hand, whirling toward me but unable to find me in the darkness. But her eyes… glow. They glow like embers, like white-hot coals. I jump back, unsure what I'm seeing.

Powers?

Was my mother… a witch?

"Moon Goddess," Thisbe whispers, teeth bared, "Protect me, last of my people. See me safely to Vaeloria, last of my blood, last of my name–" Her voice tapers off as she steps into the darkness again, her glowing eyes fading into nothingness, and then she just… disappears.

I grope for her in the dark, but my hand grazes another door-knob–misplaced, like it doesn't belong here.

"What are you going to show me next?" I ask with a sigh and yank the door open.

"Where did you come from, child?" an unfamiliar older woman asks Thisbe as I step into a… washroom, a washroom within the servants' quarters of the Ebonclaw castle. Mother shivers violently in a big, fluffy gray robe while the maid brushes through her wet hair. I glance at the copper tub, the water still steaming but dark and murky with filth.

"I–I–" Thisbe clamps her mouth shut for a moment before continuing, "a village up north, in the mountains."

"The mountains?" The maid gasps, moving toward Thisbe to look her in the eyes. "You couldn't have–"

"P-please. I need w-work. I need a bed–"

"Here, put this on," the maid rushes out, but her tone is skeptical as she looks my mother up and down. "Hurry now."

I blink, and I'm in one of the servant corridors I know so well. It's the same. It smells the same, feels the same as I race after my mother and the maid who probably passed away before I was old enough to remember her face.

Warriors shout after them as the maid hurries her into the throne room where a tall man of maybe thirty is standing in its center, talking to several other important men, and I recognize some of them. My father's commanders, his Beta, his–

My father is the tall, broad man. He–he looked so different back then. Handsome and so full of life. I don't remember him like this.

His eyes lock on my mother's. The rushed conversation around them whirls, unintelligible as I'm sucked into the moment they saw each other for the first time, and he pushes through the crowd to stand in front of her, looking down at the exhausted woman who just witnessed her own mother die a brutal death.

"My mate," he whispers, shocked.

Thisbe is speechless, but her own shock radiates off her.

Father shouts for everyone, including the maid desperately trying to get his attention, to leave them. The shuffling of feet stretches into a sucking kind of silence where I can hear their hearts beating rapidly, but neither says a word for a long, long time.

Finally breaking out of the haze, father shakes his head, his lips parting in disbelief. "I've been looking for you. I've been waiting for you for such a long time."

She reaches for him, and that first touch… it's what dreams are made of.

I feel it in my chest as my heart convulses. She touches him, and he sighs like the feel of her is his undoing, and then he's clutching her, her arms wrapped around his waist as she squeezes, murmuring prayers to the Goddess we share.

"I've been looking for you," he says over, and over.

Thisbe is crying silent tears into his shirt as he murmurs prayers of thanks into her wet hair.

I close my eyes, my tears slipping free, and feel the vision collapsing around me.

When I open my eyes, I'm back on the beach of gems, watching the dark, endless water lap against the shore.

I sit down, crossing my legs, and wait.

DEALS AMONG DRAGONS

Kael

I wake in one of Ashton's sprawling guest rooms in the early hours of the morning. It's a clear day, for once. Sunlight drifts through the arching windows lining the entire far wall, making the creamy white tiles glow as I sit up, running my hand down my face. I groan into my hand, cursing myself for giving into Ashton's wine and the feast. I didn't dream last night, which feels like a night wasted.

I don't have much time to spend feeling disappointed, if not desperate, about it. I dress quickly, running my fingers through my hair to tame the curls before striding out into his maze of a palace. Women dressed in silken finery pass me with smug, seductive smiles, batting their eyelashes at me. Ashton offered to find me some company last night, but I refused. I admit, in another time, another circumstance, I would have given in.

But I haven't been with another woman since the first, clear dream I had about my mate at the piano. There were times when I could have given in, led a woman to my bed, and let the night pass in a tangle of sheets and skin. Now, even the thought of touching anyone but her makes me ill.

Ashton is equally as suspicious as he was last night when I meet him on a wide balcony overlooking several valleys below the peak of the mountain where the villages and towns spread out, their roofs glistening in the sunlight a mile below us.

"Good morning, sunshine," he grins, lounging in a chair several yards away.

"Ashton," I grumble, leaning against the stone half-wall overlooking a mile-long drop off.

"So glum in the morning," he smirks, closing his eyes against the sunlight. "And it's such a lovely morning, too."

"It's far too bright."

"We're dragons, Kael. Cold blooded. You should soak in the warmth while it's here. But, I suppose you're used to your cave of a palace and your ice cold bed."

I sigh heavily. "I'm not sure what you want from me."

"Remember who we used to do? Our nights of debauchery–"

"We were boys," I smirk, peering at him through eyes narrowed against the sun. "Now, we're kings. And you're married, with a baby on the way."

His smile is radiant–a true kind of happiness. "I suppose things do, in fact, change over the decades.

Silence settles between us for several minutes as the sun bakes the balcony. I'm not used to the heat, to the way my cheeks prickle.

"What's the real reason you're so invested in saving this wolf princess?" Ashton asks quietly, his tone edging on serious, which is very unlike him. "And don't sit here and tell me it's for the welfare of Drakthor, either. You've always turned your nose up at conflict, Kael, even before your father died, and you ascended your onyx throne. I can tell this goes beyond protecting your precious cities on the coast."

I squint at him through the sunlight as the warmth begins to seep into my bones. It does feel good, I admit.

"When you look at Elloura," I ask, "what do you feel?"

"You didn't answer my question."

"I am."

He stares at me, his brow lifting. "I suppose I feel… helpless under her spell. I wish I could let you get close to her, Kael. She's a wonderful woman. The best kind of woman. But I'd do anything, and I mean anything, to protect her. I'm afraid if you so much as looked at her, I'd lose control."

"Then you love her?"

"Yes. I believe it's more than that. You know–" He leans forward to rest his elbows on his knees, his blond hair glistening like polished gold in the sunshine. "They say mate bonds between dragons are so rare, but I suddenly find that hard to believe." He holds my gaze.

Last night, when I'd asked if they were mates of the fated variety, he'd told me they were about as close as they could get. I should have taken it for what it was–a lie. A lie to protect his true mate, a once in a lifetime opportunity for a dragon that most don't ever get to experience. I don't blame him for lying to me. He's a dragon. We're territorial, more so than the shifters who feel the mate bond similarly to us. Any other male, regardless of the relationship, is now a threat to his mate.

Even me.

Ashton can't see past that. It's biological, something woven through his veins.

"How did you know? What does it feel like?"

"Like I would die the second she left this realm," he says under his breath. "Like the idea of her in pain, or even just unhappy, is enough to make me come apart at the seams. But the… the happiness, Kael. The idea that I've found her. It's unreal. It's like the stars aligned the night we met–the night I saw her. It was a shift in the paradigm, a total departure from everything I thought I knew."

I nod, my mind drifting back to the memory of my dreams, of her, my mate. I feel like she's just out of reach.

"Now, why did you ask about Elloura?"

"You asked about the princess of Ebonclaw." I heave a breath, trying to get my mind right, but struggle to find the words I need to convey my dilemma. "I believe… I believe I have a mate out there, nearby. And I think she's in grave danger. I have these dreams, these visions of her, and recently the curse made an appearance in those dreams. Breaking the curse goes beyond protecting Drakthor from Morgathra's influence and stopping the curse from spreading to our dragon cities and towns. My mate is in danger, and the only way to help her is to rescue the princess, and break the curse."

"You'd need to find the princess's mate as well if what we discussed last night is true. That sounds like an impossible task."

"It is, but there has to be another way. The witch Annabel will help us, of that I'm certain. She's loyal to her princess, and I believe she'll help us find her mate if we rescue her from that tower."

"How is she supposed to do that?" he says with a laugh.

"She's a witch. They have their ways, I'm sure."

"And from me, you need… bodies."

"I need the full strength of your army ready at a moment's notice to join me. I need you to swear, no matter what happens, that you won't align with Titus when the war begins because there will be war."

His nostrils flare, but he keeps his gaze locked on mine.

"I'm going to get King Henry on our side as well."

"He won't agree."

"He will," I cut in, shaking my head. "If he knows what's good for him, he will. His numbers are small, but his warriors are strong. I need his army as much as I need yours."

"Are you planning to storm Vaeloria?"

"For now, I'll be sending my own forces into the village to determine whether dragon fire has any effect on the vines, see if we can get the upper hand there to slow the curse. Otherwise, there are several rural witch covens between Vaeloria and Hexeton that have remained neutral that now fall outside of Queen Maeve's magic wards protecting Hexeton. I plan to offer them safe harbor in Emerald Coast as long as they help the dragons fight, and break, this curse. The plan is already in action as we speak."

"And what will you do with the princess when you have her?"

"I'm not sure." My mind goes back to the rose scent in her room, the piano in the corner. She... can't be the mate from my dreams. She's a wolf. It doesn't work like that. It can't work like that. But I have no idea what the princess looks like. Does she have hair like spun gold? Is her skin soft, and fair? Does she really smell like roses and play the piano, or is she just the bridge to finding the woman I'm searching for and desperate to protect?

I could ask the maid we picked up from the castle, Annabel, but I wouldn't necessarily believe everything she says, and she might not trust me enough to tell me anyway.

I have another way to find that out. In fact, I've already started that secret plan in motion.

But for now...

"I have to go," I tell Ashton.

"King Henry won't take kindly to an unexpected visit."

"He won't take kindly to his kingdom falling to a curse, either. He'll need to decide between the two evils–me, or Morgathra," I reply with a smirk. "Thank you for your hospitality, Ashton. And for giving me a glimpse of your mate. She's beautiful, and you're a blessed man." I rise from the chair and walk to the stone half-wall, hopping onto it with dragon-like grace. I teeter on the edge. "I have your support?"

"Of course. Always." Ashton nods, his silver eyes glowing with the light of morning as I fall from the wall, transforming, and shoot into the sky.

The rest of my day is spent traveling into the depths of the mountains where the sun is covered by thick clouds once again. King Henry is, of course, not expecting me and not happy to see me, and sends two of his biggest, baddest warriors out to meet me in the skies just beyond his territory lines.

But I'm not a simple dragon. I'm not a warrior. I'm a king. Kings are... born, not chosen. In the days when dragons were plenty, a king could have many male heirs, but the oldest son wouldn't be presumed heir of his father's title. No, sometimes a younger son would show... certain gifts. Certain traits that made him stronger, faster, and more capable than his brothers... and he would be king by destined right– by destiny itself.

"You will serve me," I say through gritted teeth as Henry balks, his hands planted on his hips. Bloody but not beaten, I edge toward him, pointing at the two moping warriors I'd defeated and dragged back to his mountaintop palace with my talons, leaving them alive only because I need them. "You cannot throw your support behind Titus, and you know it. He will take, and take, just like he has for decades to appease the witches. His kingdom is dwindling, his people dying off. He hasn't had a baby born in Rageworn in decades, Henry. Think about it. Is that what you want for Hightower?"

"I keep my people protected just fine."

"From other dragons. But we're not dealing with other dragons right now. We're dealing with a curse that doesn't discriminate and will bleed into Drakthor in mere weeks, and then it's over for us, for our kind. Swear your allegiance to me and my cause–"

"What do I get in return, Kael? You're so young. You know nothing. You have barely lived, young king. You've never seen a real war."

"But I know," I snarl, losing my patience, "that a war between dragon kingdoms will be devastating–an extinction event, which we're already on the cusp of. You can't deny that, Henry, with the long life you've lived."

He purses his lips.

I take another step toward him. The sun has set already, and I'm tired, hungry, and ready to be home, to be done with this so I can move on to more important things. "Will you fight beside me, and King Ashton, if you're called to aid?"

"What do I get in return?" he snarls, teeth bared.

I roll my lower lip between my teeth, chuckling darkly. "Titus's territory, his people. They'll be yours to protect going forward."

"You mean to kill–"

"King Titus will never switch sides. He's loyal to Morgathra, and when the time comes, I will kill him. Relay that message if you must."

"Is that a threat?"

"His death is a promise, and in return for your loyalty, you will be king of not only Hightower, but your neighbors to the east, Rageworn. They will likely rejoice in having a new king, seeing as they are slaves to Titus and his witch handlers."

Henry can't argue with that. His eyes shine as the gears turn in his head. I hold out my hand.

"Do we have a deal?"

He hesitates for several seconds before clasping my hand.

LEGEND OF THE WITCHES

Kael

THE CITY OF STARFALL SHINES IN THE HAZE OF A LATE NIGHT RAIN shower. The rocky, barren landscape all around the sparkling city of onyx, obsidian, and silver glows under the lights of shops, taverns, and homes scattered around the city center and built into the mountains. Above, tucked in the clouds, my castle rests high above the sprawling metropolis, lost to the stars.

I pull the hood of my cloak over my head as I step out of the tunnel funneling through the mountain and directly into the city. A night market is alive with activity, and the heavy scent of roasting meat, spicy, dark tea and incense cuts through the smell of ozone as I walk through the drizzle, lowering my head against the flickering lights.

I nod as the people I pass abruptly stop what they're doing and bow. Most whisper to each other, some giggling with excitement, and others simply smile. I have a good relationship with my people. We have had several long, occasionally turbulent, but otherwise peaceful decades together since I took the throne a century ago, making me the youngest king to ascend in the history of Emerald Coast, and my father the youngest king to die, forcing me into the position before I'd fully reached maturity.

One-hundred years old is nothing in the grand scheme of things, especially considering King Titus has six centuries on me.

Six centuries he's now wasting by aligning with Morgathra, threatening to bring the rest of the dragon kingdoms down with him.

I cross a bridge over a gorge, the spray of the massive, alpine waterfall casting shimmering droplets of water over my cloak as I walk with steady, determined footsteps toward the building where the council of elders is currently waiting for my arrival.

The building is made of the same dark stone as the mountains all around me. A wide, crescent-shaped entrance looms through the rainy darkness as I approach, my boots splashing through puddles, sending ripples through my shadowed reflection.

Wide, ancient wooden doors open on their own accord, and the sounds of the city fade into silence so thick I could slice through it with my talons. A single hallway stretches deep into the mountain that the building—a temple from an era lost to time—was built within. Soon, the hallway opens up to another cavernous room, but this one is lit by large, crystal chandeliers that tremble in a phantom breeze as I look down at the dozen or so men gathered below, all of them wearing the traditional dark gray cloaks of the elders.

Some of these men have been elders for longer than I've been alive—longer than my father, who lived to be three-hundred, was alive.

A dragon has to reach five-hundred years old to be considered an elder, which is a feat in itself. These men have seen it all—lived through five-hundred years, plus, worth of our kind's history… but one man has seen a thousand years and is still standing.

Elder Atticus turns to me and bows deeply, his frail form and nearly white hair drowning in his gray cloak. The other elders follow, bowing in rank, down to the youngest.

"Atticus," I say, bending deeply at the waist as he rises, leaning on his cane. I meet his milky silver eyes, knowing he can't see very well at his age, but his gaze hones in on mine.

"King Kael. We've gathered and conversed over our dilemma, like you asked."

"Good," I reply, walking to the center of the stone room and turning to face the elders as a whole. "Before we begin our discussion, I need to add that I've just returned from meeting with King Ashton and King Henry, both of which have pledged their support in the event we're called to war."

A murmur ripples through the sea of gray.

"You believe a witch's curse will lead to the dragons going to war?" one of the elders asks, his face blending with the others. I don't know all of their names. Atticus is their leader, the only one that matters.

"I know for a fact that this curse is spreading and will soon breach the sacred border between the land of Drakthor and the magical lands of the south, yes. We will have to act, if only to defend our people."

I turn to Atticus, who tilts his head like he's straining to hear. "Atticus, what have you decided?"

I came to him days ago, before I left to try to sway Ashton, and then Henry, in my favor. Henry was a tough egg to crack, but he's a timid dragon with the smallest kingdom, and he knew better than to trust Titus in the end.

Titus has no idea I have their support. Not yet. But soon, he will, and I expect him to retaliate.

My meeting with Atticus had been about… something else. Something else entirely.

"You asked the council if dragons can be fated to anything other than their own kind," Atticus booms in a craggily, ancient voice. "We have conferred and have an answer for you."

A weight lifts off my chest as I tuck my hands behind my back, lowering my head in anticipation of the answer.

"We do not know for sure."

I look up with a frown. "That's your answer? With all your shared knowledge–"

"What we do know, Your Highness," he cuts in, taking a step toward me, "is that the occasional... witch or shifter female would have been used for breeding purposes in dire times. You know how our population fluctuates." He shrugs one narrow, bony shoulder.

"That practice is no longer legal," I growl, arching a brow, "and hasn't been since you, Atticus, were a man of barely one-hundred."

"As such," he says, waving my comment away, "the practice, and the ritual sacrifices of maidens from ancient Vaeloria and Hexeton that were common during those times, produced... strange offspring. Dragons, yes. There were very little differences between a dragon born to full-blooded dragon parents and those born to, let's say, a human mother. Maybe a slight weakness in the body, a delay in development or the emergence of their dragon forms–"

"Get to the point," I insist.

His milky, nearly blind eyes meet mine. "The true hybrids–the half dragon, half shifter or half witch offspring... those were a threat. Powerful, dangerous, impossible to control. There were several hybrid dragon kings during my childhood, incredibly, but their rise to power was the dawn of a turbulent reign that shaped our world into what it is now. The witches and shifters to the south had been sacrificing their maiden daughters to our kind for hundreds of years and revolted eventually. The dragon kings saw the dangers of hybrid-mutants, they called them–rising to power, tainting bloodlines."

"You haven't answered my question," I growl, my voice booming through the meeting hall.

"I'm getting there, Your Highness," he replies calmly and leans on his cane with a soft groan. "You asked if dragons could be mates with anything other than our kind, and yes, it is possible, but extremely rare. Even before my time, there wasn't a single shred of rumor, or written word, about it."

My nostrils flare as his words drift over my skin. "And would a... would a set of mates, perhaps, a dragon and a shifter, be a threat to the witches at all?"

The elders murmur as a group, debating their answer, but Atticus remains silent, his eyes still holding mine.

"Yes," he says as his companions settle into silence. "Yes, the witches would take that as an affront. They're particular about their bloodlines. It's how they pass down specific traits and powers. Each coven has its specialty. They're likely more lax than they once were, though. It's been centuries since I've set foot in the magical lands, you know."

Pieces of the puzzle fall into place, but not entirely. Not enough to give me a full answer.

"There was once a great coven," Atticus says dreamily, smiling around the memory as it slides behind his eyes, like he's turning the pages of a book. "They were... impeccable healers, those witches. They lived along the base of the mountains of Drakthor, the closest coven, but their relationship with the ancient kings was one built out of respect, not fear. They'd often send their healers into our mountains to assist with births, injuries, and illnesses, and in return, we'd give them our scales to use in their medicines and spells. It was a peaceful union, and the ancient kings have no written history of ever demanding sacrifices to ensure the safety of their coven from the dragons."

I narrow my eyes when Atticus sighs like the memory has turned dark, twisting through his age-addled mind.

"There are no longer covens that close to Drakthor." I take a step toward him.

"No, there wouldn't be. If there were, they'd be living in secret. Those lands are cursed now. The banished witches turned that beautiful, magic forest into a vat of dark mist and death. But once, that golden coven was our friend, our ally."

"What happened to them?"

"I don't know."

"Did they... were there any unions between the witches and the dragons that produced heirs?"

"One, long ago, yes."

His companions murmur in shock, all eyes locked on their leader.

"Long before even my time," he confesses. "There was a child born of the coven whose father was a dragon, though what kind of dragon and where he hailed from, I don't know, but there was a family line established, and the witches born of that line were rumored to have powers of light, of life itself. They're gone now, like the rest of the hybrids and the families they started."

Ryker's voice tickles my brain as he calls out to me through the mind-link, asking if I've returned from my journey into the mountains of Drakthor yet.

"Thank you for your time," I say with a deep bow.

The elders bow, but Atticus remains leaning on his cane, bobbing his head instead.

It doesn't take me that long to walk through the city. It's nearly morning now, and the market is nearly empty, only steaming stalls and air spiced with coal. I shift, my simple cloak shredding into ribbons as my wings expand then pull in tight. I power through the heavy clouds toward the peak where my palace comes into startling view against the sunrise. The thick rain clouds hug the mountains just below the windows sticking out of the rock.

I might actually see the sun today.

But what I really want to see is *her*.

Ryker meets me on the landing platform, but I wave him away, telling him gruffly that I'll meet up with him in an hour or two, once I've had some time to rest and recharge. In reality, I'm itching to fall asleep, to dive into the dreamworld again–to find her.

I have to know who she is... because if she's the princess in the tower, I'm about to risk going to war to free her.

A LIFE FOR A LIFE

MAXIANA

I'M ON THE BEACH AGAIN—THE BEACH OF GEMS AND STARLIGHT. I'M NOT sure where I go when I'm not here, but I think I might be... dying, to be totally, completely honest. I can't find my way out of this place. The beach is endless. The water remains shallow and still with no current driving it. I must be on an island, trapped on all sides, and the sun doesn't rise or fall.

I am just languishing in the dark, slowly forgetting who I am. I can't even remember my own name. Isn't that insane?

I roll a polished sapphire between my fingers, curling my digits around it, letting it warm in my hand before throwing it as hard as I can into the water. It silently skips across the glassy surface then disappears without a sound.

I close my eyes, wondering if another vision will find me. Praying the man returns to at least keep me company... but I haven't seen him in a long time, I think. I'm not sure if he's real or if he's a figment of whatever dreamscape I'm trapped in. I'm not sure if he exists outside of this place, but I'm hanging onto hope that he does because I... I know him. In an intrinsic way. A spiritual, mental, and physical way that defies the laws of time and space all together.

Because I know, without a shadow of a doubt, that he's my mate.

"Find me," I whisper into the darkness. *"Please."*

I'm answered by my own echo, like usual.

I lie back against the gems and shut my eyes, reaching for a deep, dark kind of sleep just to pass the time, but when I open them again, I'm... in the castle in Ebonclaw, and it's a warm, late spring day. Cherry blossoms fall from the trees outside the ballroom, carried on lilac and wisteria scented breeze. A younger version of my father paces incessantly, repeatedly running his hand down his face until his skin is flushed red. I watch him from an archway, and I can feel the stress and tension hanging in the air between us. I've never seen my father act like this. He's the most kind, jovial man I know. He's constantly smiling, but now? Here, what must be... two decades ago, I imagine? He looks like his world is crashing down, and within seconds, I realize why.

An older maid rushes in. "Your Highness—"

"Any change? How is she?"

"She's resting now, but I'm afraid she's still terribly ill."

He shakes his head. "I don't understand. I have the finest healers in Vaeloria tending to her. Why is she—why is she still so sick?"

The maid, who I don't recognize at all, licks her lips as she steps forward, bowing her head in submission. "The healers have mentioned her condition is worsened by her advancing pregnancy, Your Highness. She's choosing the baby over herself, trying to give the child more time before birth, but I'm afraid that time is coming soon."

"What do you mean?" Father looks up from his hand, his eyes dark and shadowed by grief and confusion.

"She's quickening, Your Highness. The baby will come within days. It's much too early—"

"What can be done?" he says, his voice edging on pleading. I can see his thoughts written along the sharp planes of his handsome face. He's absolutely distraught. He feels helpless, lost and unsure if he'll wake up tomorrow to sunshine or if the day will bring rain and the news that he's lost both his mate and their child—a child they longed for... for years.

"We can only pray," the maid chokes out before bobbing into an unsteady curtsy, her face twisted with grief as she rises and hurries away.

Father is sick of praying, it seems. He stares out one of the windows, his chest heaving with each unsteady breath he takes. His hands curl into tight fists at his side when he exhales long, and slow, having made his decision in silence.

He rarely ever spoke about the witches. I always assumed he danced around the subject. While he trusted Queen Maeve and had wonderful things to say about Hexeton, he made it very clear to me that I was a shifter, and we shouldn't ever meddle in witch business.

But today, he's choosing to meddle.

The vision blurs, the ballroom replaced by gnarled trees and gray daylight whispering through thick, unending fog. Father's boots crunch over fallen, dead branches that turn to dust in his wake, but he knows where he's going. His steps are sure, his body rigid, as he moves into a clearing, and the fogs rolls out, revealing six witches in dark cloaks, their hoods shadowing their faces.

All but one.

"It's not often we have the honor of hosting a king in our coven," Morgathra says as she bows low, her black cloak picking up dirt and leaves as she rises. She has raven black hair so straight and thin it's easily picked up by the lightest of breezes that snakes through the forest all around her. Her eyes are dark and glassy—a very dark shade of green, I realize. She's odd looking. She seems so young—her voice is so lifted and lightly seductive when she speaks, when she greets my father with another dramatic bow, that I would assume she was my current age, maybe even younger than that. She has the voice of a maiden but the face of an old crone.

I glance around the clearing at the other witches. I can only see their marionette mouths and gray, sagging skin along their jawlines. Wrinkled necks, long, gnarled fingers. Ancient women, indeed.

But when I turn back to Morgathra, her eyes shine a brighter green. It's a familiar color, but I don't understand why.

"She's sick," Father explains, his voice low, pleading. I must have missed the beginning of their conversation because I find it hard to believe that Morgathra would know who he was talking about, but she seems familiar with my father in a way that goes beyond royal formalities. "There's nothing more the healers can do. Queen Maeve won't help. I've already sent word to Hexeton that we're looking for a cure for her illness, but she keeps her healers on such a tight leash."

"What kind of sickness is it, Your Grace?" Morgathra asks, tilting her head to the side like a bird. She looks like an owl, actually. She moves as silently, as gracefully, as the illusive creatures of the night. "How did it begin?"

"She was well two days ago. Everything was fine, but then she collapsed in the garden while tending to her roses. We couldn't wake her. She burned with fever for two days until it broke, but now she's wasting away, using the last of her strength to try to keep the baby alive."

"The baby?" Morgathra smiles wickedly, and my stomach curls. How had he not sensed this when he was here, all those years ago? I watch my father bow his head to hide his desperate, overflowing tears and see the smirks on the other witches' faces. A few of them lick their lips like they're starved. "Tell me, Your Grace, where does your Luna hail from? Is she not from Ebonclaw? Your females are the hardiest shifters, the best mothers. Why is she failing when others have not?"

"She's not failing–"

"This pregnancy is killing her," Morgathra cuts in darkly. "You must be honest with me, Your Highness. Has she not been ill this whole time?"

"It was a hard pregnancy, yes, and we tried for years before she came with child–"

"Ah," Morgathra says, clicking her tongue. She glances at the other witches, who return her knowing gaze with their own. A shiver runs up my spine as the memory of my mother running for her life when her village was attacked echoes through my head.

My mother wasn't just a shifter. She was a witch, wasn't she?

And somehow, Morgathra knows that. "A hybrid pregnancy is terribly unsafe, my king. You should have come to me sooner–at the very beginning." She extends her fist, unfurling her fingers one by one. Hazy green light expands from her open palm before fading and twisting into something new–a tiny glass vial full of liquid the same color as her magic. "This will strengthen her and the baby. They will live."

Father steps forward, too far gone in his own desperation to question what's inside, but she curls her fingers around the vial, shaking her head.

"How much for it? I'll give you anything."

"Anything?"

"I have gold. Riches beyond your wildest dreams. I can build you a castle–"

She steps forward, eyeing him, walking a circle around him as her minions begin to shuffle in her direction. "I have a question for you, Your Highness, and you must answer honestly. If you had to choose between them–your mate or your child–who would live, and who would die?"

"My mate would live," he says without hesitation.

She smiles like this was the answer she was hoping for. "This potion… it will save your mate, but its magic is very strong. It may be too much for the baby, I'm afraid, but if she's as ill as you say, it's the only thing that'll save your mate."

Father is on the verge of collapsing. My chest convulses as I watch him make the worst decision anyone could possibly face.

"I'll give this to you in exchange for the child," she says, walking another circle around him. "Should the child live, it'll be so weak and ill it won't live for more than a few hours. I want it. And you will bring it to me."

"I can't–"

"You can, and you will, if it means saving your mate's life, won't you?" She has him backed into a corner. He eyes the vial now dangling between her fingers.

"What do you want with a dead baby?" he asks through hot, suddenly angry tears. "What will you do?"

"Nothing. We'll bury it in our own way, like is customary of our kind. But… you mentioned how hard it was to achieve the pregnancy in the first place. I have potions for that."

My skin crawls when I realize what she's insinuating. Potions made from… from a child.

"No," I whisper into the vision, shaking my head at my father. "Don't accept her terms. You can't!"

But Father takes the vial from her and slides it into his pocket before wordlessly turning from the witches and walking briskly away, the fog rolling in and covering his body in a blanket of silver.

I wait to be transported through the vision again, to see him giving my mother the damning draught, but I remain in the clearing, and when I turn to the witches, all eyes are on me.

Morgathra smiles directly at me, and I realize she can see me. She knows I'm here.

"You're so beautiful, little witch." She smiles, her teeth a thick, grisly yellow in the fading daylight. "I knew you would be. You must know what he does next, don't you?"

My nostrils flare, but I keep my mouth pinched shut. It's hard to do, honestly, given that I can smell her stink from where I stand. They all reek like rot and death.

She steps toward me, grinning from ear to ear. "He'll give her the potion and damn her to eternal rest before you're even born. Your mother never got to look upon your face, *Maxiana*."

My name. She said my name. I remember it. I have to keep remembering it…

"You should have died with her, you know. That was my original plan. That failed, obviously. You're likely not aware of what happened next." Her smile turns sinister as she slowly moves toward me. "I came to collect, but he'd burned your mother's body against the custom of your people, knowing I'd want her bones. He refused to give you to me, saying you'd lived when I'd said you wouldn't. He said our deal was broken because your mother died."

"And it was," I tell her, but my voice shakes with fear as she bares her terrible teeth at me.

"I cursed you, Maxiana. Your kind should be dead, every last one of you. I thought I'd done it, eradicated the filth of the golden witches when I discovered their last stronghold and rained hell upon every man, woman, and child… but your mother survived. Your fool of a father came to me, falling into my trap. It wasn't hard to curse your mother's roses. The golden witches were so gifted in gardening, you know. Or, maybe you don't know because your father never told you anything about your mother–your real mother. The witch."

"She wasn't a witch."

"Ah, but she was."

"She could shift–"

"A trick of the mind, my darling. A flip of the wrist. Your mother was a liar, a schemer, and she deserved to die just based on the blood running through her veins. You will perish, as well, you stupid girl. You are so blinded by your own beauty that you can't see the dangers all around you–like me and them." She motions to her minions with a sick, twisted smile. "Your bones will be ground into ash. Your skin will be dried and used for our potions–our elixirs of youth and beauty. Just like your ancestors were, when they'd fall into our traps, and we'd flay them apart, using every part of their bodies to strengthen our magic."

My stomach curls painfully. "No–you won't. You can't–He–"

"He?" she echoes, arching a brow.

"My–my mate will come for me."

"Really? Silly girl, believing a mutt like you could have a mate."

"I see him. He's coming. He's going to save me. He'll save me from whatever you've done!"

Something clicks behind her eyes. First, she looks confused, but then… I realize I've said too much. Far too much.

I close my eyes, begging to be sent back to the starlit beach.

"Be weary of that man, Maxiana. He's not what you think he is."

I open my eyes to nothing but darkness, and for once, feel relieved to be trapped within it again.

SAY YOUR NAME

Kael

I SLIDE MY LEGS FROM BED, RUBBING MY EYES AS RAINY MORNING daylight floods my room. The arching windows cast shadows as rain coats the glass, sending a thrum through the space. But when I rise to my feet, dressed in nothing but a pair of undershorts, I see her and know at once that I'm still dreaming.

Thank the old gods for that.

She's not sitting at the piano at the corner like usual. Her face is shielded by her hair as it falls loose over her shoulders, curling softly in ribbons of gold and the palest of blondes. She crosses her arms, hugging herself, dressed in a thin, cream colored robe of silk, the same color as the nightgown that brushes her ankles.

"What's the matter, my love?" I ask, internally debating moving toward her. All I'd have to do to see her face would be to smooth her hair away, tucking it behind her ears.

She shakes her head, looking down at her feet. A tear drops and lands on her robe, sinking into the fabric and leaving a wet stain.

"What happened?"

"We're dreaming. You know that?"

"Yes," I admit, swallowing past the growing knot in my throat. My body's reaction to her sadness is almost painful. I want to rip the room apart, put a hole through the stone with my fist out of anger for whatever, or whoever, made her cry.

"Do you know who I am?"

"Look at me," I whisper, edging a single step in her direction. "Turn and look at me. Let me see your face."

"I can't," she says, her voice strained. "I'm afraid this vision will fall apart the second I see you, and I've been waiting to see you again." She trembles, hugging herself tighter. "I—are you trapped here, like I am?"

"No, I'm not."

"You can wake up from this, then?"

"Yes," I answer, only a few feet away from her now.

"Where am I now?"

I take a breath, trying to calm myself down enough to touch her, comfort her, however she needs it. "You're in my home. My room."

"I can't see anything past the clouds."

"It's because this castle is in the clouds. Built into the mountain, at its peak."

She whips her head in my direction, and I freeze. She, too, realizes what she's just done, and a look of panic blurs her... devastatingly beautiful features. She's... breathtaking. Perfect in every way. Her face is soft, delicate, her cheeks full with youth and eyes wide, round, and the purest, most beautiful blue I've ever seen.

I know her lips from memory. They're as plush, wide, and soft as my body remembers. But they're a beautiful, soft rose color, just like the stain on her cheeks.

I hold her gaze, afraid that the second I blink or look away from her, the dream will fade, and we'll be ripped apart again.

"I think we're okay," I say after several heart wrenching seconds.

Her chest rises and falls rapidly with shuddering breaths, her eyes still full of tears. "I'm afraid."

"Why? Because of me?"

She shakes her head, her eyes holding mine in the exact same way—like she's worried blinking will break the vision. But I'm shirtless, and in the soft glow of the stormy morning light the shimmer of scales are evident behind my skin. My dark, nearly obsidian eyes are probably glowing faintly in the light. I probably terrify her.

"No," she whispers, lowering her arms. She extends a trembling hand, and I step toward her, closing the distance between us.

A sense of relief sweeps through me the moment we touch. I finally risk closing my eyes, unable to help it, as her fingertips ghost over my forearms.

"What is this? Under your skin?"

"It's who I am," I breathe, lowering my mouth to her hair and inhaling deeply. Roses, like usual. My favorite scent. "I'm a dragon."

She's quiet long enough I start to worry that when I open my eyes, she'll be gone, but when I do, she's slowly, carefully, wrapping her arms around my bare waist, pressing her body against mine.

I knit my fingers through her hair as she unravels, silently crying against my skin. Her tears are warm, and her mouth moves against the muscles of my chest but no sound comes out, like she's praying.

I close my arms around her and pick her up, carrying her to my bed. I lay her down, sliding in beside her, and cover us with the blankets.

Minutes pass like this in silence, nothing but the sound of the rain patting against the window to break the stillness in the room. She moves her hands up and down my stomach, her fingers tracing the swirls and lines of my interlocking tattoos.

"What are you afraid of?" I ask.

"I can't get out of this dreamland. The beach of gems and starlight? I'm trapped there. I think—I think someone put me there. But I remember my name."

I stiffen for a second, jolting back to sudden reality. For a moment, I feel the dream trying to pull away but yank on it, yank on the bond between me and this woman.

"Don't tell me yet."

"I have to," she whispers. "I need your help."

"Are you the princess of Ebonclaw?" My voice wavers. I feel that sick, twisting sensation start to funnel through my body, through the marrow of my bones. Dragons are… territorial. Deadly when crossed, but damning when their mates are involved.

"Yes."

I close my eyes as the urge to shift, to shatter this dream and go to her, her real self, her cursed body trapped in that tower, nearly sends me over the edge.… But we're here now, together. I'm not sure how long we have been like this, and I know I'll spend days begging the gods to bring me back here.

Every day that passes inches closer to the full moon. I can't miss my shot at saving her, at breaking the curse, but I know better than to act hastily. The closer we get to the full moon, the longer Morgathra has to stretch her powers. She's growing weaker by the day, I'm sure, trying to keep the curse at its full strength, to keep it spreading.

"You're my mate," I say, rolling over to face her. My nose brushes hers as her eyes flutter closed, a soft, mewling sound leaving those beautiful lips I'm desperate to kiss. "I know where you are. I know what happened to you, and I will come for you. You have my word."

"She knows about you."

"Who?"

"The witch. Morgathra. She did this to me. She killed my mother. She killed my mother's people first, but my mother got away and found my father. I–I'm the last of my kind."

"You're a shifter."

"I am, but I'm not. She was a witch. I had no idea."

The dream starts to fade, the corners of my room growing hazy, like a fog is rolling in.

I clutch her close, whispering into her hair, "Tell me your name. I want to hear you say it."

"Maxiana."

"Maxiana," I breathe, clothing my eyes as the dream begins to shatter. "I'll find you. I will save you. I will see you soon, for real. I promise."

Her warmth is replaced by nothing–just stale, cold, morning air. I open my eyes to my room again, but I'm alone, and any warmth and light that was here only seconds ago is gone, replaced by gloom and rain.

But the scent of roses hasn't left my skin.

I leap out of bed and dress. It's early enough that the maids and servants I employ aren't even awake for the day, but I'm not in need of breakfast. I walk through the castle, weighing my options, fighting against the urge to end this–and now–but by some miracle from the gods themselves, Ryker is maneuvering the same long, rounded corridor, walking right in my direction.

He pauses, surprised to see me awake.

I pause, shocked to see him half-dressed and sneaking out of Annabel's room.

He rolls his lower lip between his teeth, letting it go with a pop. "She needed–needed an extra blanket."

"Did you use your body heat to keep her warm through the night instead?"

Guilt momentarily flashes behind his eyes before he grimaces, caught red handed.

"The witch isn't a toy to play with while she's here, under my protection. I thought I made that clear."

"Annabel," he cuts in sharply, hackles raised, "is not my plaything."

My brows arch. I sense that same predatory drive in him that I've been fighting since I was lost in another dream with the princess. Ryker widens his stance without realizing it, puffing up, attempting to dominate me with his body in a way that tells me if I even look at Annabel's door, he'll try to kill me. Right now, he's not seeing his Alpha standing yards away. He sees me as a threat, regardless of my station over his.

"She's mine," he asserts after the space of a breath. "She belongs to me and me to her."

"I see."

"You don't. She's my mate."

"Oh–"

"I don't care if you don't believe me. If you want to punish me, so be it, but I will duel with you if you even–"

"You're fine, Ryker. I'm happy for you."

He blinks, staring at me in shock, but doesn't relax.

"I believe you."

Now he just looks confused. He relaxes just a touch, rolling his shoulders and looking suddenly boyish. "You don't think it's odd. Me being mated to a witch?"

"It's odd but not impossible, I've learned. In fact, the Elders told me this can happen. I'm not in a position to question them, given that… I have found myself with a mate, as well, who is not a dragon."

Ryker eyes me cautiously, the two of us obviously trying to come to terms with what this means.

"Who?"

"Take a wild guess." I continue walking, brushing past him. I can feel him eyeing me with heated violence as I step past his mate's door, but that tingling feeling that warns me I'm in grave danger eases when I put a decent amount of distance between me and the barrier.

Eventually, he follows, saying breathlessly, "Do you mean…. You can't mean–"

"The princess of Ebonclaw. I'm the one who has to break the curse, and I have a feeling Morgathra knows that now. If she isn't planning an immediate attack on our territory, she will be soon, which means we have to act. We only have a week until the full moon."

"What do we do?"

"We're going to invade Vaeloria, like planned, but soon. Tonight, if I can get King Ashton on board. There's somewhere I have to go first."

I cross into the training hall where the stairs leading up the flight deck bloom into sight. Rain drips down the steps from the open, circular hole in the ceiling. I turn on my heel to face Ryker, who looks slightly pale and confused.

"Annabel… I'm guessing she's going to be staying here, with us, for the foreseeable future?"

"Her entire life, yes."

"Well, in that case, find better rooms for you two—one of the old suites. Move her in with you and keep her close for the next few days. Wait for my word. If Morgathra attacks in my absence, do what you must to protect Starfall."

"Where exactly are you going?"

"Queen Maeve," I tell him with a sigh. "I want her on our side, or out of our way, when I bring this war to her doorstep."

BELLADONNA

Kael

AN ENTIRE DAY PASSES AS I WAIT FOR WORD FROM THE WITCHES OF Hexeton. I'd sent flyers–dragon warriors–into the skies to deliver a message for the queen–a summons.

If she accepts and agrees to meet with me, it will mark the first time in over five hundred years that a king of the dragons and a queen of the witches have stood on the same plot of soil and spoken. I'm aware of how momentous this is–not just the threat of the curse, but me breaking from the choking grip of Titus's rule over Drakthor.

Ryker paces near the spiraling staircase leading up to the landing platform. It's pouring rain, of course. There's a bite in the air tonight that's not usual for this time of year. It causes my skin to prickle, pebbling with gooseflesh as I wrap my arms tighter around my chest and lean against the wall.

"They should have returned by now," Ryker growls, losing his patience as thunder rumbles all around us.

"It's the storm. Starfall's socked in. There's no way around it.

They're probably hunkered down in a valley nearby until it passes," I remark, but the words sound hollow. I'm not sure I believe them.

I roll my shoulders and debate what to do next. We're running out of time to wait around, to hope the queen decides she should involve herself. Morgathra's curse is spreading beyond Vaeloria now, based on reports from the scouts I've sent flying over the town every day for the past two weeks. The vines now stretch into the forest, covering every building and small village they've met.

One glance at Ryker tells me everything I'm thinking, and feeling, is validated.

I kick off the wall and stride toward the stairs, stretching out my shoulders and flexing my back as I let my powers take over. "Stay here. Have your men stationed on every peak around Starfall."

Ryker nods, but his face is cast in serious shadows as he watches me climb the first few steps.

I continue, "Send four warriors to Terminus and deliver a message to Ashton. Tell him this is happening now. Once I've met with Queen Maeve, we will invade Vaeloria and end this."

"Do you have a plan?"

"No. But I'll call on you when I'm done in Hexeton. We're going in and rescuing the princess regardless of Queen Maeve's involvement." I look down at him as I reach the final steps. Rain pelts the back of my head as I conclude, "Have every warrior and able bodied man prepared to fight in the event Titus makes a move on Starfall in my absence. Prepare for that like it's already happening. Bring the women into the caves near the base of the valley and keep them there. The city of Starfall must be cleared out completely by morning. Am I clear?"

"As crystal," he replies, bowing his head ever so slightly.

"Make sure Annabel is with the other women. She'll be safe with them." I turn toward the gaping hole in the ceiling, climbing the final steps into the downpour. I shift, tearing my clothing to ribbons, and shoot into the sky.

Thunder and lightning battle around me for what feels like miles as I try to fly above it, where the oxygen is thin and the air so cold ice begins to form along my back and wings. I can only fly this high for so long. The cool seeps through my scales and penetrates my muscles, numbing my bones until I start to lose feeling along my spine.

I keep moving, beating my wings as I glide on top of the massive, whirling cyclone moving directly into the dragon lands. It's not a normal storm. Not at all.

Green lightning sizzles beneath, crackling as it splits the clouds, sending a rush of air toward me. I glide around a dome of angry clouds, unsure how long I have at this altitude, but I'm not risking diving any deeper than this.

The hours' long journey is cut in half at this rate of speed and how high I am, and when I dip back down into the storm, the raging, mystical woodlands spread out below, cloaked in shadows and torrential rain. What used to be creeks are now rivers. Landslides spill gray, inky mud into the water, turning the ribbons that weave through the forest black. Green lightning erupts behind me, sending a sharp wave of electric heat in my direction, but I dodge as I dive lower, my talons grazing the tops of the highest trees.

A whizzing sound breaks through the storm the second Vaeloria comes into view. An arrow grazes my left wing, but I manage to roll just in time to stop it from going right through the paper thin, fibrous skin. I set my sights on Vaeloria, fighting rain and utter darkness as more arrows whiz through the forest. The city is completely covered in vines now. Several buildings are crumbling from the tight squeeze of vines now as thick as old growth trees.

But I'm still half a mile away, and what was once a thick forest of dense greenery is choked by the curse. Vines lift from the tallest trees, tendrils reaching for me as I glide toward the city, narrowly missing arrows that whiz beneath me.

A vine catches my tail and coils upwards at an insane rate of speed. I thrash, snapping out of its hold but more vines reach from the trees, catching my talons, roping around my ankles. My wings expand and pull in tight repeatedly while I try to stay airborne, but it's no use. I crash into the trees, sending splintered pieces of wood and debris flying when I hit the forest floor.

I'm immediately surrounded by figures in dark cloaks. Some carry smoldering torches that fizzle in the rain while others carry lanterns with strange, swirling light within. My dragon form twists into my human form, and then I'm on my hands and knees, soaked, and coated in my scale-like armor as black as the woods all around me.

One of the figures steps forward, carrying a torch. Magic curls around the flickering embers to keep the flames lit, which illuminates her glassy, almost silver eyes. She's remarkably beautiful, but I know it's a trick. Her wide, full lips painted a deep, blood red lift into a vicious kind of a smile as she grins, "King Kael. What an honor it is to have you in our forest."

Panting, struggling to catch my breath, I rock back onto my knees, letting the rain wash over me. I wasn't planning on coming face to face with Morgathra's coven today... but the opportunity presented itself, I'm not going to let it pass me by.

I could end this here–and now.

But this witch isn't Morgathra.

"Are you Belladonna?" I ask, my voice like gravel.

The woman's smile widens, revealing sharp, white teeth. "My reputation must precede me, Your Grace."

"Where is your master?"

"My queen? She has better things to do than hunt dragons."

"I only have time and words to spare with her. No one else."

"You'll be pleased to know that soon you'll be before her, and you can pledge your loyalty to her cause face to face. She's been waiting, you know. King Titus said the other dragons would bend the knee, but so far, she's been kept waiting for the rest of you miserable lizards to even acknowledge her."

"A king does not bend the knee."

Her smile flickers, the corners of her mouth turning inward into a frown. She scans my face before turning ever so slightly to a nearby witch and nodding. Every witch in the clearing moves in on me. I don't fight them when they use their powers to create cuffs of iron around my wrists. I taste the magic on my tongue as they force me to rise. It tastes like blood–rich and heady, like liquid copper. A sheen coats my mouth, making me slightly dizzy, but I move with them without fighting, each step carrying me closer to Morgathra and the end of this curse.

I can kill a witch. I'll decapitate her and return to Drakthor with her head as a trophy. I'll send it on a mount to Titus as a little gift, I suppose, before Ashton takes over his territory and displaces the cowardly king.

A sharp ache explodes through my back when the forest opens up to nothing but empty, rolling hills of gray, dead grass. I fall to my knees, biting down on a scream as something sharp and angled drifts over my spine.

Belladonna giggles as she steps ahead of me, inspecting a curved blade of sorts. Lightning flashes, giving me a single glimpse of the weapon before darkness takes over again, and it's enough to make my blood run cold.

"This is my favorite blade," she explains as the witches circle around me again. "Do you know what it is? It's a dragon talon, shaved down to be flat, but it maintains its ridge. I see how sharp your talons are. I'm sure Morgathra will have uses for yours."

"And his scales," another witch chimes in.

"And his blood!" another exclaims.

Belladonna snaps her fingers and a hovel appears, a trapdoor lifted by two witches that must lead deep underground. My breath catches in my throat as I eye Belladonna wearily. "Where are you taking me?"

"To our coven, of course. We have so many plans for you, King Kael. Morgathra will come to see you once the curse reaches its peak, but until then, you're mine."

A ripple of excited laughter simmers behind me, but I ignore it, keeping my eyes on Belladonna instead. "Fine. Show me your coven. I hadn't realized you burrowed underground like insects, but it makes sense."

She scowls at me before two of her witches try to pull me upright. They struggle against my weight, but I don't help them at all. Shuffling through the trap door, my back throbs with searing, heated pain. I can feel blood trickling into my armor with each step I take, following a long walled in tunnel. Everything is stone–ancient stone. Whatever this place is was built long ago and taken over, I assume.

Doorways begin to flood into view. People stick their heads out–witches, all of them. Some are young looking while others are horrifically old–nothing but skin and bone as they step out of their caves to join the precession.

I'm herded into a wide, cavernous space lit but lantern fire. Cauldrons boil over large swatches of shimmering embers, scenting the space with spices I can't even begin to name. It's ridiculously hot here, even for a dragon. Sweat prickles along my brow as I'm roughly shoved to the ground and rolled onto my side. Several women rush toward me, clawing at my armor, but Belladonna hisses, baring her teeth at them.

"Everyone will get a piece of him, that's a promise. But for now, he's mine. Everyone out!" she screams, and the witches scatter, murmuring insults and making their disappointment known.

I rise on my elbow, fighting against a fresh wave of hot, seemingly unending and depthless pain, and look the witch in the eyes.

"You're making a mistake keeping me down here," I tell her, smiling wryly.

"You're bound with iron. You won't be able to escape this place, and if you were thinking of traveling into Vaeloria, think again. You can't get past it. The vines will drag you down just like they did your warriors." Her smile turns deadly as my stomach turns. "We have plans for them, too."

"Are they dead?"

"Not yet. You're more valuable to us alive as it stands."

"For what?" I ask, glancing around the now empty space.

She kneels in front of me, tucking a lock of my hair behind my ear, and digs her long, sharp, absolutely filthy nails into the underside of my chin. "Babies, Your Highness."

She lets me go and begins to shed her cloak.

NOT MY PROBLEM

Kael

Belladonna shimmies out of her cloak, revealing a lithe, curveless figure. I watch magic glimmer over her skin as the cloak falls to the ground in a puddle at her feet, her narrow body covered in nothing but a slip that's seen better days.

I laugh at her, shaking my head as she reaches for my cuffs. "Babies? You think I'll willingly fuck you, witch? Is that what you're planning to use us for? Breeding? Are you that weak as a people? Will no other men fuck you?"

Her magic ripples over my skin, leaving me momentarily numb. I can't move when she takes off the cuffs, smiling wickedly as she rolls me onto my back, and I'm paralyzed.

"Dragons are strong and long-lived. Your scales make our magic, our potions, more potent. Your bones are hard as diamonds and make for the best weapons. Your blood keeps us young," she draws out the words in a seductive hum. "And… yes, Your Highness, we want you to strengthen our coven. Imagine the children we could produce together."

"Get off me."

"Don't act like you don't enjoy it," she purrs.

I can't move. My body won't react as her fingers glide down my arms. My armor still covers me, but I can feel the bite of the stone on my back where she flayed me open with a dragon talon.

"I refuse. I won't allow you to do this, to me or anyone else."

"You don't have a choice." She smiles, throwing her dark hair over her shoulder. She runs her hands down my chest and the sensation jolts me back into full awareness. I jerk, sending my powers of transformation flooding through my body, and in a twist of scales and dragon fire, shift into my dragon form.

My back injury splits, and my human scream becomes a roar laced with fire that scorches the room. Belladonna is engulfed, and the sound of her pain is brief as my fire tears through her, turning her beauty back to what she truly is–an ancient, wrinkled being, just like the rest of them.

Witches are supposed to be mortals. They steal our magic to lengthen their lives… to restore their beauty. Her gnarled frame fades into ash and embers as I whirl, my tail knocking over the cauldrons, spilling their contents onto the floor at my feet.

Other witches storm into the room before quickly retreating as I barrel toward the hallway I know leads back outside, but I won't fit in my dragon form.

I shift back, and the pain is worse than before. My back is horribly injured now, but I can move. I run as best I can, knocking over any woman who runs in my way, trying to stop me.

The second my skin touches night air I shift again, and my vision blurs with pain.

"DON'T LET HIM GET AWAY!" someone shrieks as the first arrows begin to fly. I can't keep myself high enough. My talons graze the tops of trees as vines start to snake from the tallest branches, reaching for me again.

Vaeloria comes into view once more. The witches must have built their cover nearby, using what seemed like the basement level of an old temple as their base.

A vine catches around the tip of my tail, momentarily causing me to lose my balance. I careen to the side, snapping the vine, but six arrows puncture my left wing, one right after the other. My roar of pain echoes off the distant mountains, cracking over the thunder.

More arrows burst through the trees as I sail over the old stone wall that serves as the boundary between Vaeloria and the forest. The arrows pierce my belly and chest this time. Most of them bounce and splinter against my thick, rock-like scales, but one manages to pierce me at the juncture of two scales–a soft spot–a weak spot.

Pain like I've never felt before jolts through my body. My vision blurs as hot, sharp agony fills every vein, carrying to every muscle, and settles deep in my bones.

My left wing is weak, and I'm flying sideways when I coast past the castle and dip down into the city proper, and further, until I fly over Vaeloria altogether.

But I'm... drifting off course. Hexeton is southeast of Vaeloria, only a few miles of forest and roads between them. I can barely see a thing. My head pounds, and my mouth fills with the taste of metal. Blood sprays when I roar in warning to the warriors that appear below me when I descend into the outskirts of Hexeton. I planned to land at the castle in the distance resting atop a tall, gradual incline, but I'm starting to fail, starting to fall, and can't beat my wings. In fact, I can't move. I can't feel a thing as the ground comes closer and closer, until I land face first in a long patch of grass just beyond the walls of Hexeton.

My body curls, my neck bent at a terribly painful angle as I skid across the grass, leaving a deep imprint and pulling up dirt and rocks in my wake. My vision tunnels, and my ears ring as muffled shouts of alarm bounce through one useless ear and out the other.

With the last of my strength, the last of my dwindling powers, I shift back to my human form, my battered scales becoming armor that covers my legs, torso, and arms, and I roll to a stop.

I look up into the rain as darkness creeps in, my vision fading at the edges with each desperate, strangled breath I take. The arrow is still fixed in my chest, stuck between my ribs. I imagine that pinch I feel is the poisoned tip scraping my heart–not deep enough to pierce it, but close enough to kill.

Shadowed figures rush toward me. Men, it seems. Men and wolves. I grab the arrow with the last of my strength and pull it out, blood spraying.

A warrior in Hexeton garb kneels, grabbing my shoulders.

"I'm here to see the queen. I demand an audience," I croak, my vision fading to the point I can't make out his facial features. Everything goes black. I take a shuddering breath and let myself slip into the dreamworld.

Soft voices whisper nearby. I'm not sure if I'm dreaming or not when I open my eyes to slits. I'm in an unfamiliar room full of smells and people I don't recognize. Three young women gather in a group at the end of my long, narrow bed, whispering rapidly to one another before one of them notices me opening my eyes, and pauses.

She rushes to my side when I try to sit up, but I... can't. I can barely move. My finger's twitch, and her voice is slurred, like she's talking underwater.

She turns to her companions and seems to shout an order that has them darting out of the room. I close my eyes again. My mouth fills with blood. It takes all of my strength to reach up to feel along my chest to the arrow wound, but it's covered by thick, slightly damp bandages that wrap all the way around to my back, which is numb.

But I feel... lost. My powers are gone. I couldn't shift if my life depended on it. Judging by the light coasting through the room, it's... morning, but how many days have passed?

"Leave us," a deep, rumbling female voice commands.

The young woman trying to tend to me immediately obeys, her soft, soapy scent replaced by something heavier, something more spiced and rich.

A shadow passes over me, blocking the light flooding my eyelids, so I open my eyes with some effort and find a very tall, very regal woman of middle age looking down at me with her head tilted to the side, her wide, blue eyes peering down at me with marked disapproval.

Queen Maeve's dark red hair falls over each shoulder in a thick stream of crimson silk. She's just as grand and beautiful as I've heard her described.

"I didn't expect you to live this long," she says without a hint of emotion in her voice, but a slice of curiosity weaves through the words.

"How long have I been like this?"

"Two days," she answers, tilting her head to the other side as her gaze drifts over my chest.

"How long–how long until the full moon?"

She licks her lips, her eyes roving up my body to meet mine. "It'll rise in full tomorrow night."

"You have to realize what's coming. You have to know."

"The curse? I have Hexeton guarded by my own magic."

"It's not enough."

"You dare question the queen of the witches?"

"Do you know what that coven is doing, Queen Maeve?" I ask, barely able to keep my eyes open and locked on her face. "What they plan to do with the dragons? They want to use us as–as breeders, for one. Then our bodies as ingredients for their potions and spells–"

"What makes you think I care about the fate of the dragons?"

"You have to care about the future of your own people. Morgathra wants to end you, too. This curse is going to come to Hexeton. You know it. I know it. You have to stop it."

"My people are protected by my powers. I suggest you do the same for yours."

I lean my head back, staring at her through slits. "What does Morgathra really want?"

"What every banished witch wants. More power." Queen Maeve turns to the window. "She practices blood magic, which is banned here. Banned in every coven, in fact. This curse... I'm not sure it can actually be broken."

"What do you mean? The princess—"

"Ah, the princess," she whispers. "The one who started this mess. The poor, innocent child? She's likely dead already, so there's no point. I have to do what I can here, in Hexeton, and for the mortal lands to the south. The shifters of those territories are already preparing for whatever war comes. But we do not need the dragons involved."

"I came here to speak to you—"

"You came to beg for my help, and I have to refuse you. The witches and the dragons broke from each other, and so it will remain. I will not subject my people to sacrifices and rituals of old."

"I'm not asking for that."

"Then why are you here, if not to use this curse as a loophole to reinstate the dragon claim to my skies?"

"My mate," I whisper, my voice cracking as my body throbs with agony. "I have to find her. She's in Vaeloria. She's in the tower."

Queen Maeve turns to me, shaking her head. "Impossible."

"I can break the curse if I can get to her. My warriors will come. The warriors of King Ashton and King Henry will come. There will be war in Vaeloria. I can't promise it won't spill into Hexeton. What side will you be on? Mine—or Morgathra's?"

"Neither."

"That's not an option," I say with a wince as fresh pain slows my heartbeat.

"You're dying," she says with a soft, almost uninterested sigh. "These injuries are… fatal, I'm afraid. I cannot help you. I do not have what my coven needs to safely heal a dragon. You are too late to break this curse. I have no interest in involving myself."

"You would let an entire city fall to another witch queen?"

"She is not a queen. She is an imposter—"

"And if you sit back and let your own people suffer, you are just as bad as she is."

Through the glare of the sun, I see the queen's eyes narrow into cat-like slits. She considers my words for a moment, tilting her head from side to side. She moves in a dreamlike manner, and for a moment, I think I might be dreaming. This pain is almost too intense to be real. This feeling like I'm constantly slipping away and clawing back again… it's like something from a nightmare.

"We'll meet again when I wake," I tell her. "When I wake from this horrible dream."

"You are here, in reality, I'm afraid," she replies. She turns back to the window with another soft, breathy sigh. "If you survive until nightfall, I will help you. But I will not aid you in this war."

"Help me how?"

My eyes close on their own accord, and I'm pulled into the shadows, swept away on a wave of pain. I succumb to my injuries, letting myself drift, praying I wake up in time to save her.

To save my mate.

GOLDEN LIGHT

MAXIANA

THE BEACH OF GEMS IS ROILING WITH AN ENERGY I HAVEN'T FELT HERE before. I can't explain it, but everything feels... wrong. I rise from the sparkling sand of tiny stones, crossing my arms over my chest against a sudden, unusual chill. A soft fluttering breeze rushes toward me, disturbing the otherwise calm, inky-black water. The wind carries whispered voices that make my skin pebble–voices of pain and suffering, of utter despair. A male voice, calling out to me in the stillness, my name a whisper, a prayer, a rushed apology.

I furrow my brows as the breeze ceases and silence returns, but that chill remains, licking up and down my spine while I turn to inspect the never ending beach.

There's a door again.

Unease creeps through my body, weaving through my veins, as I stare at the heavy, stone entrance to another vision, I'm sure. I'm also not entirely certain I care to see what's on the other side this time, not after witnessing my father making deals with the witches... deals that must have trapped me here.

The pieces of the puzzle are beginning to click into place, I believe. I'm not dead. I'm not asleep, either. I'm suspended in an in-between, unable to escape, and I know the witches who tricked my father are to blame.

But the visions are coming from elsewhere. It's another thing I can't possibly find the words to explain, but I feel like I'm being tugged toward the door, like whatever's throwing me a lifeline in this storm wants—no, *needs*—me to see what's on the other side.

"I'm growing tired of this," I whisper to the magic all around me, taking a shuddering breath. "I just want out, okay? I want to go home." I curl my arms around my stomach and take several steps in the door's direction before hesitating. I can see the details of the portal to who-knows-where from this distance. It's an unusual shape—an arch, with a sharp, angled tip where a crest is engraved in onyx. A dragon curls around itself, eating its own tail. The moon cycle surrounds the dragon, and on the face of the door, the night sky is carved in delicate detail. Constellations bloom as I run my fingers across the surface. It's warm to the touch, beckoning me, and the door slowly creaks open with the slightest pressure from my fingertips.

Warm sunlight spills over my bare toes, and I'm in that room again.

His bed is large—the biggest bed I've ever seen. His bedspread is black with soft, silken silver sheets, which matches the rest of the details of his room. Large, beautiful stained-glass windows let in just enough sunlight to illuminate his body in the center of the bed.

I close the door behind me, but he doesn't stir.

We had a dream together recently. I'd been here, looking out the window, trying to find familiarity in the valley below, but this place is… ancient. Older than any of the castles and villages in Vaeloria.

But even though the details of these dreams with him are beginning to be clearer, I can't remember his face.

He's lying on his side, turned away from me. My fingertips brush over the footboard as I round the bed, keeping my eyes on him, noticing that he's barely breathing. He's asleep. He doesn't know I'm here.

What was his name? Did he ever tell me?

He told me something, but I… I forgot. It was important. It was something about him that… that didn't make sense. Something that reminded me that this is all a dream.

I walk to his side, pulling down the sheets enough to see his profile. He's… he's the most handsome man I've ever seen. His dark curls brush his shoulders as he lies prone, folded into himself almost like he's in pain. Dark lashes flutter against his high, sharp cheekbones. His nose is straight and regal, and his lips?

I brush my fingers over them, praying I remember him when this vision fades again.

Sunlight stretches across the room toward us, illuminating his skin. I swear on the Goddess I see the outline of scales beneath the surface. They glimmer with power, barely visible to the naked eye.

"You're a dragon," I whisper, my breath catching in my throat. "I–I remember. I remember you told me that."

He doesn't stir. He doesn't so much as make a sound as I inspect him, my hands dusting over his cheeks and jaw in a featherlight touch. My fingers drop to his neck, then his chest, where roping, swirling tattoos begin. His body is painted like the night sky–full of stars.

I begin to tug the sheets down but stop, my heart jumping into his throat. I yank on the sheets, pulling them down to his waist as my blood begins to rush in my ears.

"No," I croak, "No! No, no, no!"

Blood seeps into the sheets, into the mattress. Thick, dark, angry blood that spreads beneath him in a sea of crimson. A wound near his heart gapes, and his back is torn like someone took a knife to his spine, flaying him open like a fish.

I stumble back in horror, shaking my head, tears beginning to spring along my lower lashes before diving free, leaving silver streaks on my cheeks.

"Wake up!" I shout, shaking, unsure what to do. I cover my eyes, trying to break the vision myself. This is just a nightmare. This isn't happening in his real life. The witches are tricking me, aren't they? This isn't real!

"WAKE UP!" I scream, both to him and myself, but when I drop my hands from my face he's still there. His dark eyes are open now, looking right at me.

A choked sob ties a knot in my throat I can't swallow past as I fall to my knee on the side of the bed. His arm stretches across the mattress, reaching for me. I grab his hand, knitting his fingers in mine before bringing it to my cheek.

"I was hoping I'd see you again," he says with effort, his voice strained with pain.

"What happened to you? This isn't real, is it? This is just a nightmare?"

He smiles sadly, his eyes shining with what I can only describe as grief. "I'm going to find you when I get better. I have a few days–" He grimaces then coughs. Fresh blood floods the mattress beneath him. His coloring is off–pale, nearly gray.

I clutch his hand, my tears sinking into his skin. "You're dying!"

"I'm fighting it."

"What can I do?" I lift my cheek from his hand to look around the room, desperately trying to find anything to press against the wounds, but the corners of the vision are already fading, turning back to starlit darkness. "Please! What can I do?!"

"Just look at me. Let me see you."

I hold his gaze, my chest convulsing as his fingers go cold as ice. I can feel him slipping away. It leaves a gaping hole in my chest, like he'd filled some void, and now he's just... just fading from my grasp.

I feel it then. I know who he is. I know why he's in my dreams. I know why I've been dreaming about him for months now, his figure always blurred by the night sky. "You're my mate," I whisper as my tears blur my vision.

Another sad smile touches the corners of his mouth. "Yes. I am."

"You can't die," I beg, shaking my head. "I don't even know your name!"

He squeezes my hand. "Kael."

"Kael," I echo, my eyes creasing as his name leaves my lips. "I'll remember it. I'll remember you. But you have to keep fighting, okay? Please!"

"I'm tired," he admits, his eyelids fluttering.

I shake my head when his grip on my hand loosens. "No—no, Kael, stay awake. Stay with me, please!"

He takes a shuddering, painful breath before his eyes close, and that void in my heart widens as if in warning.

My scream can be heard in the heavens. I'm sure it splits the sky into pieces. I'm certain my tears could flood valleys, bloating streams and rivers as they move toward the sea. My grief turns to anger—anger at being trapped here while he dies. Anger at being helpless. Anger at knowing I'll never meet him in our real life, and whatever future we could have had is now gone, erased before it could begin.

I clutch his hand, screaming with all my might as that anger turns to… determination. Something clicks in my brain, my body. Something warm and powerful that floods me with heat. Something bright and rich, like liquid gold, and suddenly the room begins to spin, and Kael's cold, nearly lifeless hand still entwined with mine warms again.

I hadn't realized I had my eyes closed until a bright light explodes beyond my eyelids. I open them to slits, panting as ribbons of golden light shimmer through the room. I open my eyes wider in pure shock as the light weaves between our joined hands and travels under his skin, illuminating every vein, every scale. He winces, arching off the bed with a breathy gasp as the beams sizzle over his chest, and I… let go of his hand.

I stumble backward, my back hitting the wall as I watch the horrific, deadly wound on his chest knit itself together again.

I look down at my hands, panicked, as golden light simmers at my fingertips. What have I done?

How did I do it?

"Kael?" I whimper, looking up at the same moment the vision falls apart, swirling into darkness once again. The beach expands before me, faint starlight replacing the cozy, stone interior of Kael's room. I blot my tears, whirling in despair as I search in vain for the door, for the way back to him.

But a soft glow radiates all around me, turning the glassy gems beneath my feet to shining stars that look like they were just plucked from the heavens. Light fills my eyes as I bring my hands to my face, stifling a gasp. My hands glow like–like gold. Like the stars flickering overhead. My fingertips are laced with what I can only describe as magic that weaves between my fingers and down my wrists, pulsating under my skin in time with my thundering heartbeat.

The light fades, but my chest is so tight I can't fully fill my lungs. What have I done? What did I do to him?

What does this mean?

A soft creaking sound like a door opening whispers out behind me. Slowly, I turn, my skin erupting in gooseflesh as another door appears just a few feet away. It opens wide, straining against its hinges.

"Where are you taking me this time?" I ask the nothingness all around me, like anyone can hear. Fear stops me from taking a step. I'm frozen in place as the door beckons, spilling hazy, warm light toward my toes. "Bring me back to him. I don't want to know anything else. Please!"

The door remains open, but my body won't move.

"Just bring me to my mate," I whisper, another tear sliding free and trailing down my cheek. "That's all I want. Please. *Please.*"

Slowly, as if pulled by a phantom wind, the door begins to close. I'm on a precipice. Wherever I am… I'm not supposed to be here. I'm trapped. But something else is here with me, something that's also not meant for this place. It's trying to help me, I think. It's trying to show me things I need to know to fight my way out or to help the man my soul is connected to.

I leap toward the door, grabbing the knob before it can close all the way. I yank as hard as I can, and stiff, warm wind rips toward me, lifting my hair from my shoulders.

"I need to get a message to him!" I shout, holding onto the door-knob for dear life as the magic within tries to pull me into the void, into another vision. "Tell him about the tunnels you showed me. They lead into the castle. Show him what you showed me!"

I'm ripped from the door, which closed with a booming echo behind me.

PROTECTION

Kael

I jolt into awareness, blinded by startlingly bright sunlight in an unfamiliar room. I have to blink repeatedly to clear my hazy vision while reaching desperately for the woman who'd just been kneeling beside the bed, her hand clutching mine. I grope thin air, grimacing against a sharp rush of heat that funnels through my body like a snake, slithering through my veins. It… hurts. Hurts like hell, actually. The heat is nearing a boiling point when a sharp yelp booms nearby, followed by scuffling feet and the sound of something shattering on the ground. The light abruptly fades as curtain rods squeal against metal, and then someone's touching me, speaking so rapidly I can't make out a single word they're saying.

A small, warm hand presses against my forehead then releases, and then I'm alone again, but this time in the dark, which is a welcome relief. I struggle into an upright position, my chest and back aching, which is a reminder I'm horrifically injured, but… I smooth my hand over my chest and find nothing but skin–nothing but heated, feverish skin that glows a faint gold.

I look down, my eyes going wide as a pulsating ripple of golden light floods through my body before dispersing.

The door opens again before I have a chance to come to terms with what's happening, and I'm abruptly reminded of where I am and under whose care.

Queen Maeve's shiny red hair ripples as it slides over her shoulders, her heart-shaped face washed in shock as she hurriedly rounds the bed. Several maids follow her inside, all of them wearing similar expressions of surprise and awe as another, final, burst of light travels under my skin and settles deep in my chest, causing me to huff a breath full of tight pain.

The queen's eyes move from my chest to my face.

"What did you do to me?" I grind out, smoothing my hand over my bare chest—where the wound should be, but now it's completely healed. This woman told me she wouldn't help, that it was likely I wouldn't survive the night, but here I am... and one glance at the curtains and the light peeking through the folds of fabric tells me it's morning.

"What power is that?" she says breathlessly, her eyes going suddenly milky and glazed. Her fingertips glow as she reaches for me, but I slide out of bed, stepping out of her way, towering over her.

"What did you do?"

"Nothing. This was not me or any of my witches."

I'm wearing undershorts but nothing else. I look around for anything to wear, meeting the eyes of one of the maids, who squeaks and hurries for the door, hopefully to find me some clothes.

All the while, the queen watches me move across the room. I can feel her gaze on my back as I pull open an armoire and fish for a shirt. I find a robe instead, which is long enough to cover most of my body, at least.

"You said you have dreams of the cursed princess," the queen says under her breath as I turn around, tying the robe in place. "Elaborate."

"That's none of your business."

"Did you see her while you slept?"

I look the witch up and down. I don't like the look on her face. It's a hungry kind of look, something that immediately sets me on edge.

"Did she do this for you?" she presses, taking a single step in my direction. She lifts a hand, dismissing her maids.

"Do what for me?" I ask, but my senses are haywire. The dragon within me recoils from the witch, trying to warn me to keep my mouth shut.

"This," she says, motioning toward my chest. "That was a very… very rare type of healing power. Something I thought was long extinct."

"Maybe one of your witches has the ability and treated me in secret."

She shakes her head, just once, but she hasn't blinked in a while. She holds my gaze, her body rigid and on the defense. Her posture makes my skin tighten with the threat of transformation, but I keep my dragon powers contained… for now.

"She did this for you, didn't she? The princess of Ebonclaw? You must tell me the truth."

My lips tighten into a smirk. "I'm not telling you anything. You have been unwilling to help my cause at every turn. You're not my ally."

"I brought you here, into my home, to heal–"

"You were letting me die," I cut in, and she pales, but her eyes shine as they hold mine.

"I cannot risk a war. My people–"

"You and I have that in common. But instead of sitting around and pretending like this curse isn't coming for my people, for my kingdom, my cities and villages, I've chosen to do what I can to protect what's mine."

"And that includes the princess," she whispers, as if to herself. She finally blinks and turns away, her fingertips grazing the curtains.

The heat in my body begins to fade, and I feel… normal again. Whole and strong.

"If you know something, you need to tell me," I demand, but the queen just smiles slyly, shaking her head.

"But first, you have to tell me how she did this."

"You're so convinced it was her."

"Those powers have been gone for twenty years," she rasps, baring her teeth. "Only one coven possessed them, and they were eradicated by Morgathra and the dragon king you call Titus."

"What?"

She nods, that sly smile fading. "Morgathra's magic of choice is dark, King Kael. She was like me and the other witches once–young, beautiful, and powerful, but she chose dark magic over the magic of light, of air, water, and earth. She chose blood magic, chose to use her powers for evil. When I rose to power, I had no choice but to banish her and her followers. I should have known back then that not killing her would come back to haunt me, but I made vows to the Goddess that I would only use my magic for good, and I still stand by that."

"You had a chance to kill her, and you didn't take it?"

"It would have made me just as bad as her–"

"You have to know what she's capable of. Why didn't you stop her in the beginning?"

"Because she–she was more powerful than me," she admits, and it looks like it takes a great effort to do so. "But our magic isn't all powerful. It fades, you see. The more we use, the more it dwindles. Using dark magic drains her rapidly, but there was one thing that kept her, and her coven of darkness, young and powerful."

"Dragon scales."

"Yes," she nods, her voice low. "Dragons scales, dragon blood, dragon bone. She killed so many of your kind during her first years. You weren't born yet, but I remember it clearly. We once lived so peacefully with the dragons."

"Was that before or after you sacrificed your own young maidens to the dragon kings?"

"It was a sacrifice to continue protecting us from our enemies, which included Morgathra." She steps toward me, her chest rising and falling in a sharp breath. "And you must know by now that those sacrifices didn't always end in their deaths. In fact, many went on to have children with the dragons. Some even fell in love." Her eyes meet mine. "And, their lines... their magic, intertwined with the dragons, creating something new."

"That was happening long before Morgathra."

"Yes, you are right, but she was threatened by it. The covens of dragon ancestry were a threat to her dark magic. They were born of magic of light, of life itself, a kind of magic that rivals mine. She killed them all–found their last coven and killed every man, woman, and child, and used King Titus and his warriors to help. There was nothing left of that coven–not even their bones."

I grind my teeth as she walks a small circle around me.

"But I believe one witch survived. The timeline is perfect. The coven fell just over twenty years ago, and the princess is... twenty-one."

I feel my wings beginning to materialize against my will. I have to protect the princess. That's the only thought in my mind right now.

"Whoever did this to you comes from that coven. Was it her? The princess?"

"That would be impossible seeing as she's currently cursed and dying while you sit here, twiddling your thumbs."

"She comes to you in your dreams, doesn't she? You are connected that way. Mates."

"I'm not speaking of this to you."

She smiles, chuckling faintly. "Dragons are all the same. You hoard your powers and your mines, your gems and precious metals that us witches could use in potions and for our powers. You've always been that way–so territorial–so terrified of other's trying to claim what's yours. A mate is no different to you, is she? She is the treasure you wish to horde–"

I catch Queen Maeve by her thin neck. She stills but doesn't look panicked, so I tighten my grip until she lets out a shaky breath.

"I will bring war to your doorstep if you even look in her direction," I growl, unable to stop myself from confirming what she already assumed. "I will kill you. I will flay your skin from your body and hang it from your palace like a flag."

"She needs protection. I can offer that," she croaks.

"She is mine. She does not belong to you and never will."

"She is a witch, King Kael. She will never truly belong to you."

I let her go. She takes a steady step away from me, ignoring the red mark left on her neck by my grip. She reaches into her gown, pulling out a chain. An amulet hangs on a string of pearls and black diamonds.

She slowly, carefully, places it in my hand, curling her fingers over mine. "I can't offer you aid. I won't involve my witches, my warriors, or put Hexeton at risk. But I can offer you this. It's powerful. There is a protection spell on this amulet. No harm will come to you as long as you wear it. If it's broken, the spell will be rendered useless, so be careful."

"I don't trust you."

"You must, because if this princess is truly what I believe she is, her death means the end of her line… the end of the specific power. The dragon ancestor who passed these gifts down to their mortal line… well, those types of dragons don't exist anymore. Princess Maxiana is the last of her kind."

I search the queen's eyes. "What type of dragon?"

"A Golden Dragon. They were gone long before you were born, King of Thunder and Night." She squeezes my hand then whispers, "Protect her. I will not take her from you. You have my word."

She steps away, disappearing into a haze of mist. The door opens to a terrified maid who drops a pile of clothing on the ground and scurries back out of the room.

I fist the amulet, rolling it over in my palm before setting it down to dress. After several minutes of thought, I put the amulet on, tucking it into my shirt.

I find my way out of the castle. No one speaks to me. In fact, they hurry out of sight as I pass, my wings erupting the second I step over the threshold and into warm, midday air. The moon is visible–full and bright, even against the blue sky. In a few hours, it will reach its apex, the curse will be permanent, and Maxiana will die.

I cannot let that happen. This ends now. Today.

'Send in our warriors,' I say into Ryker's mind, praying he can hear me. Then I pass the guards along the edge of Hexeton and step into the plains between Queen Maeve's coven and Vaeloria.

A TRAP

Kael

I WALK INTO VAELORIA THROUGH THE MAIN GATES THAT FACE THE ROAD to Hexeton. I let my wings erupt but keep the rest of my dragon form at bay, for now. I need to conserve my strength. The sun is high overhead when I reach the ring of vines as thick as tree trunks. I have no way in unless I fly, but the amulet around my neck is a constant reminder that I may have a sense of protection now, but if it breaks… which shifting into my dragon form will no doubt do… it will render it useless.

I squint up at the top of the gate where the vines curl around the iron, twisting it into unrecognizable metal.

But the vines don't reach for me here. In fact, I can lay my hand against a vine, and its tendrils don't burrow through the wall it's built.

I wonder if the amulet is to thank or if the curse has reached its peak, slowing as it passes into its next phase with the coming of the full moon.

I can't climb this wall. The vines twist and coil tight, creating a flat, impenetrable surface. I make the snap decision to take off the amulet, fisting it between my fingers, and shift, tearing through the borrowed clothing as my scales ripple over my body. The second the amulet falls from my claws, the vines uncoil in a great, thunderous screech that makes my ears ring. I burst into the air as the first tendrils of vines stretch toward me at a great rate of speed, but I'm airborne and faster than them.

They're everywhere–covering the roads, the little villages that lead to the city proper. Even the old growth trees are bent and splintered under the weight of the vines. Small houses are nothing but rubble. As I soar over the outer ring of the city, large buildings stretch toward me, vines lifting from the roofs and chimneys. The castle comes into view along the horizon. Storm clouds gather in the distance with the promise of rain. I send another message to Ryker, knowing that at this point, from this distance, he'll hear me, and within an hour, my dragon warriors will descend on Vaeloria.

But there's not much any of us can do until I find Maxiana and break the curse.

A vine catches around my tail and tugs me off course. I'm tossed to the side, taken aback by the strength of the vine, but it releases me, sending me tumbling through mid-air toward the forest again.

The vines shrink back toward the buildings when I regain my speed, coasting along the outer ring of the city instead of cutting straight through toward the castle, but I need a way in.

The wall around the castle is totally blocked.

I tuck my wings in tight and whirl toward the castle at a high rate of speed. When I leave the forest and begin flying over the inner city again, the vines stretch and snap toward me–at me, slicing across my scales. Thankfully, I'm moving too fast for them to do any real damage.

The tower sprints into view as the storm clouds roil, beginning to cast a long shadow over the gnarled forest beyond Vaeloria. Waves of rain ripple through the forest, cutting through funnels of smoke I hadn't noticed before. In fact, the sudden bursts of wind carried by the storm bring noise with it, war cries, and my body tenses as figures begin to move through the trees like shadows, chasing…

I roar, expanding my wings as I skirt the side of the castle, my talons scraping over the vine-covered roof of the tower. Twelve dragons pierce the clouds as lightning flashes across the skin. Arrows shoot from the forest but miss the dragons as they dive toward the city, talons outstretch and claws ripping vines from the walls, the roofs of buildings. I join Ryker's ranks. He's a large, black dragon, like me. Dragons with powers of thunder, of storms, of lightning.

We meet each other's eyes as we soar in a large circle around the city, dodging vines.

'There's at least a hundred witches coming toward the city!'

'They have arrows but are armed with their magic. Do not get shot down,' I tell him.

He roars, alerting his men to a change in formation, and our entire group dives back toward the forest.

I open my jaws wide and send a burst of flames into the woods, scorching trees and earth all the same. Arrows whizz past me, grazing my wings, but now the rest of the dragons are raining fire on the witches, who dart away but regather the moment we turn back toward the city.

"Continue scorching the forest. Chase them off."

"What about the city?"

"Leave it to me." I lean to the side, splitting from the group. In the distance, green light begins to weave through the forest, following a group of what I assume are witches coming to aid their coven.

I careen back toward the castle, dodging vines while looking for a clear place to the land. The castle is totally covered–there's no way in or out.

I spot a clearing in the woods on the left side of the castle. I dive toward it, shifting into my human form before my talons even touch the ground. My scaled armor covered my body to the neck as I roll to a stop, jumping to my feet, and whirl.

Vines move like serpents in my direction, sliding and slithering over the wall. My only option is to climb. I have to do it, and I'm more spry in this form than in my dragon form. I have to try.

I race toward the vines, leaping over them, sprinting as fast as my feet can carry me while the roars of my meager forces split the sky like booming thunder. Vines lash at my legs, but I step around them, trying to close the distance between me and the wall, the wall that would otherwise not be a problem–but now?

I jump over a tangle of writhing vines. I'm only a few yards away. Weaponless, I just need to get over the wall. I'll worry about the vines later. I need to get inside the castle. Once I'm inside, I'll find my way to the tower.

I remember the thick vines blocking the entrance to the tower and wince, momentarily forgetting my footing, and a vine juts out, slapping across my thighs and twisting painfully.

I grunt with effort as I'm lifted and tossed like a rag doll. My body collides with a tree before falling with a crunch. The air leaves my lungs in a whoosh, but I don't have a moment to catch my breath before vines clutch my ankles and drag me back toward the wall. I dig my fingers into the soft, damp ground, but the vines are too strong, too tight. I try to shift back to my dragon form, but... I can't. The vines are magic. They're cursed, and it's preventing me from using my powers. That has to be the reason.

But then my fingers catch something metal. I grip what feels like a handle. The vines jerk me backward, dragging me further, but I keep my grip, holding on with both hands. A trap door of some kind groans as the force of the vines pulling me away wrenches it open. Dust puffs into the air. A stale scent fills my nose.

A tunnel system. I've seen this before, haven't I? Why is this familiar?

A dragon's roar pierces the air and sudden heat barrels toward me in a wall of thick, silver flames.

I bow my head, gritting my teeth as heat that would burn the common man to a crisp rushes over the top of me, but I'm not a mere man. My scales turn bright red under the fire's heat, but the vines loosen, screeching as they let me go and pull away from the flames that roll past me toward the wall.

I look up, panting, as a silver dragon soars over the forest.

"Took you long enough," I grumble, knowing Ashton can't hear me, but it doesn't matter now. He's here, and based on the twenty or so silver dragons he brought, he's ready for battle.

I grip the trap door and pull myself upright. The vines snake toward me, squealing in a high-pitched, ear bursting shriek that makes my skin tingle with disgust. I jump through the trap door, swallowed by darkness, and pull it closed before the vines can reach me.

The only thing I can see is... inky darkness. The vines slither over the door, looking for me, unable to figure out where I've gone. The sound of their snake-like tendrils coiling over the metal makes my stomach pitch, but I swallow back my unease and turn into the darkness, lowering my arm from my nose and breathing in stale air.

No one has been down here for... decades. No light nor sound has breached the tunnel walls. Stone—wet, moss-covered stone. Water pools over my boots as I move forward in a straight line, the sound of the vines replaced but my footsteps. I walk several yards and look up, which doesn't take much effort. I have to bend to fit in the space, but I imagine I'm passing under the wall now, walking in the direction of the castle.

Grates open up overhead, covered in vines, but the first inklings of late afternoon light trickle down, illuminating the tunnel that leads through the streets surrounding the castle. Soon, the light is gone completely, but something shimmers in the distance. Golden light flickers from a grate at what seems like the end of the tunnel, where an old wooden door comes into view.

My heart hammers as my dragon senses start flaring to life. I can taste the gold nearby. It's a dragon sensation. We're built for mining, able to find the most precious minerals and gems... and something exquisite and powerful is mere feet from where I stand, crouched, my back beginning to ache.

My fingers slide across something smooth, and I pause, turning to find the gleam of gold I noticed just a moment ago.

A sword... I think... is stuck in the wall. Its hilt is just visible, jutting from the stone, like whoever left it here tried hiding it. I pull with all my strength, but it barely budges.

Again, I yank on the sword, but I need more than this human strength…. If I shift, I risk collapsing the tunnel on top of me, trapping myself here.

"Come on," I growl, pulling with all my strength, grunting as the sword moves enough to knock some crumbling brick from its resting place.

The vines covering the grate twitch, however. I look up, watching them recoil, showering me in sunlight. I yank on the sword again, pulling as hard as I can manage as the ends of the vines pull back over the grate and stop, pointing down.

"Fuck," I whisper, trying to still my thundering heart.

The vines burst through the grate. I scream with effort and pull the sword free. Metal sings as it splits the air, cutting through the waterfall of vines like warm butter. They screech, dripping green fluid as they sizzle back out of the tunnel, and I run.

I don't bother opening the door. I clutch the sword as I burst through it, landing in a basement storage area. I crash through crates and boxes of molding produce, knocking over kegs of beer and barrels of wine in my haste to reach a twisting stone staircase leading up to the castle proper. Springing upward, I reach the first level of the castle—a maze of servants' quarters, hallways, and the main kitchen. Vines cover every inch of the level, but the sword...

I slash through the vines, groaning and grunting as I send it flying, ripping through walls of vines. I have no idea where I'm going, but I'm desperate to move up and take the first stairwell I find, slicing through vines as they snake toward me. They're nothing compared to the strength of this sword.

Coated in sweat, my arms burning with exertion, I cut through a doorway and step into a hall I find familiar. I was here with Annabel once, when she'd led me to the princess's room.

There aren't as many vines here now, which doesn't make sense.

I look around, finding the place… normal.

But far, far too quiet.

"You're too late," a female voice sneers.

I turn toward the voice, panting as Morgathra comes into view, her dark hair billowing over her shoulders as her eyes burn green.

Behind her, through a set of windows only partially covered by vines, the sun begins to set.

ROSES AND SMOKE

Kael

MORGATHRA IS BEAUTIFUL. STUNNING. LONG, STRAIGHT BLACK HAIR flows down to her impossibly narrow waist, and her skin is as pale as alabaster. I'm sure, in her youth, she was a lovely woman, but even now, with her face smooth, flawless, and young... I can see the marks of age she's failing to hide–the scars of ugliness, of evil, no magic can erase.

Her eyes are round and the brightest green I've ever seen. Green, like spring grass. Green, like the first buds on the trees after a long, hard winter.

Her eyes draw me in and spit me out, wasting precious seconds. I raise my sword, but a beam of green light flies from her fingertips as she cackles menacingly, her powers ripping the weapon from my grip.

"You fool," she hisses, lowering her arm and taking several steady, unwavering steps in my direction. "You must think yourself a hero, don't you? King Kael? The dragon king come to save the shifters from their ultimate demise?"

"What have you done?" I ask, slowly stepping away from her. Out of the corner of my eye, I spot the sword resting on the ground, vines curling around the hilt.

"You're too late to stop the curse. You could have been on my side, you know. You could have been a hero in the era of the witches and the dragons, united."

"That is not what this is." I growl, shaking my head. "Your madness is infecting what was once a peaceful, prospering city. You're foul, dark magic is a stain on what the witch queens have built and what they protect."

"And what have the witch queens ever done for your kind, dragon?" she sneers, lifting a brow. "Kept you locked away in your mountains where nothing grows and the sun never shines? You were once their protectors, their guardians of the skies but now? What are you but a speck in history, a forgotten legend of a time of rituals and sacrifices–"

"You," I snarl, taking another step toward the sword, "and your coven have been enslaving and torturing dragons for decades, using us to strengthen your fleeting powers. That ends now."

"Do you really think you stand a chance against someone like me?" She grins, lifting her hands, her green light flickering along her long, sharp fingernails.

A thundering boom shakes the castle. Morgathra stumbles, crying out as bricks fall from the ceiling, one of them striking her square in the shoulder. Her scream of agony rips through the corridor as another boom nearly brings the castle to its knees. Even her vines quake, drawing back from the sword, and I lunge.

I grip the hilt and send it flying, metal singing as it pierces thin air. Morgathra sends a beam of light toward me but misses, striking her vines instead. A dragon's roar cuts through the rumbling of the castle as if in warning before a blast of silver fire rains down through the new holes in the roof.

I have mere seconds to dodge the flames. I race toward Morgathra, raising the sword and swinging it toward her. The tip slices through the air… but she disappears in a blast of light just when it should have sliced through her neck.

More bricks fall from the ceiling, crushing vines and sending dust funneling down the corridor, blurring my line of sight. Overhead, the dust clears, and at least a dozen silver dragons pierce the sunset, sending sprays of their silver fire into the vines choking the castle.

The sky is turning a deep violet against strips of deep gold and orange. I have minutes to save her.

With new found purpose, I sprint down the corridor, leaping over vines and dodging their spiky tendrils. They lift from the ground but with less fervor. I race toward the door leading to the tower, raising my sword and hacking away at the vines. The thinner ones are easy to cut through, but not the thicker vines.

I'm covered in sweat, my dragon armor sliding over my skin with every jerking motion of my arms swinging the sword. I ignore the calls of my men and Ashton's dragons and tear through the vines. When the last one snaps, I kick down the door and run up the stairs.

Vines are everywhere. I lose my footing and slide down several feet, then begin to use the golden sword to keep my balance, stabbing and hacking the vines on my way up.

I can feel the curse in the air–a sucking, choking sensation that makes the air in the tower feel suddenly, inexplicably thin.

But the door comes into view. Vines race for it, making a last-ditch effort to stop me, but I grunt with the effort of sending the sword through the vines covering the door. Air rushes around me and the vines burst in a shower of green magic, then fall away.

The magic's pull remains, choking me, strangling me with invisible fingers as the curse reaches its apex. The door is locked tight, but I use all of my strength to shove it inward. My wings erupt, pumping madly to give me more power while thin vines wrap around my ankles. The wood splits, then splinters, and bright, golden light fills my vision.

For a moment, I think I'm stepping into that dream world again. I wait for the light to fade, to turn to inky-black, star filled darkness, but my feet remain on cool, ancient stone instead of sinking into a beach of smooth gems–and the light...

I shield my eyes from the final glare of the sunset with my arm, squinting and blinking rapidly to try to clear my view. Windows line the circular wall, all covered in vines, but they're starting to retreat, letting in shreds of sunlight and warmth.

A large bed rests along the far wall... and that's it. The room is clean, tidy, and free of vines.

I lower my arm, looking down at the rose petals at my feet.

The smell of roses is everywhere.

My eyes fall on the young woman lying prone in the center of the bed, her hands neatly folded over her chest. Golden blonde hair fans out over her pillow and the bedspread in silky, glimmering waves.

My heart ceases to beat as I walk toward her, stepping through the fading ribbons of golden sunlight. I tuck my wings in tight to fit, letting them fade away, leaving me in my human form.

She's... beautiful. She's everything I ever dreamed of. Maybe I knew she was mine long before she started showing me her face and speaking to me in our shared dreams. I look at her fingers. Dainty, long fingers I know can fly over piano keys and make the sweetest of melodies. Fingers that have touched my skin, comforted me, healed me.

"Maxiana," I whisper, nearly choking on her name.

She's here. She's here–and she's real.

But the roar of the dragons alerts me to the ever growing danger beyond the tower walls.

The sunset light creeps back toward the windows as I step closer to the bed, but then I'm struck from behind, my body careening to the floor.

I roll away as a metal pipe crashes to the ground where my head had just been.

"How dare you?" King Titus sneers in his human form, raising the pipe again, posed to strike. "You want to side with the shifters? The lesser witches? You're a disgrace to our kind!" He brings the pipe down, but I stop it with the sword, the metal chiming as they meet.

He presses down with all of his strength, but I'm younger, faster, and stronger.

I shove him off, sending him catapulting across the room. His back hits the wall with a crunch as the last light of sunset begins to fade.

"Morgathra could usher us into a new era!" he shouts, struggling to stand. "A new era of dragon leadership!"

"She's lying to you!" I bellow, edging toward the bed.

"You're the one being lied to, boy. You think the dreams you're having of this wolf princess are real? Think about it, Kael. She's a dog. You're a dragon. In what world would a dragon waste their time on something so beneath them?"

He pushes off the wall, panting, his skin shredded from several long gashes made from dragon talons. He's been battling his way through my forces to get here, hasn't he? To try and stop me?

The unhinged look in his eyes tells me he's not going to stop until I'm dead–or he is.

But then his eyes land on the slumbering princess behind me, and he raises the pipe.

The idea of harm coming to her has me rushing the elder dragon, my voice breaking in a scream of effort as I send the sword flying, the hilt leaving my battered hands.

The sun slips below the horizon as the sword crashes into the wall, slicing through Titus's chest. He slumps to the ground as the room grows eerily dark.

I stumble backward toward the bed, watching the fading light in horror. I whirl to the princess, leaping onto the bed, leaving tracks of dust and ash all over the sheets.

She's… she's starting to grow cold like her skin is turning to stone.

"Maxiana," I breathe, gathering her limp body to my chest. A puff of air leaves her lips in a frigid wave of mist, but she doesn't open her eyes.

What if I'm not her mate? What if I've wasted all this time chasing a delusion? What if Titus was right, and the witches planted those dreams in my head to try to buy themselves some time?

But somewhere in the distant recesses of my mind I hear that song, those sweet, delicate plucking of keys. I feel warm sunshine on my face as I watch her comb through her golden hair with her fingers.

She's mine. In those dreams, she was mine.

I claimed her as mine.

I'm a dragon.

We don't like people taking our things.

I press my lips to hers as moonlight begins to creep through the tangled vines covering the windows.

At first I feel... nothing. I feel nothing but soft, full lips against mine. She smells like clean sheets, like roses and soap. It's a familiar scent, something that ignites a fire deep in my bones as I clutch her closer, my heart shattering with every passing second.

I'm too late. I'm far too late.

The full moon rises on Vaeloria while I hold Maxiana to my chest, whispering against her lips.

"It's me," I tell her, my voice cracking. "It's Kael. I came for you. I swore I would. I'm so sorry. Max, I'm sorry. Goddess—" I press my lips to hers again before nuzzling her neck, breathing in her scent.

Maybe she wasn't my mate. Maybe I was wrong, but... I can't let her go. My arms tremble as I graze my teeth along the delicate skin of her neck, tasting her, silently begging her to wake up.

Beyond the tower walls, the battle continues now plagued by darkness. Smoke fills the air, cutting through the heavy fragrance of roses as fires burn all over Vaeloria.

I'll go into the flames willingly. I'll sacrifice myself to whatever cause is left.

I just can't accept that Morgathra won...

I bite down on Maxiana's neck. It's impulsive and reckless, but I'm being driving by pure instinct as moonlight drifts onto the bed, spreading silver beams across her legs, then her stomach.

I feel it then—that pull. That binding of the threads between us.

Dragon's don't bite to mark.

The marks are already there, branded against our hearts. I feel the brand that the Goddess pressed to my soul when I was made sizzle to life, ignited by the threads binding me to this wolf, this shifter princess, and feel the room around me begin to spin.

I was right.

She's my mate. She's my–

Maxiana takes a shallow breath before opening her eyes against the moonlight.

AM I AWAKE?

Maxiana

The pebble-like gem's glisten in the starlight, like always. I sit on the beach where still, star filled water reflects... nothing. It's so quiet today. I've seen no more doors, nor had more visions, for Goddess knows how long.

I toss a gem into the water where it bounces, creating little ripples that stretch the stars reflected on its surface. I grab a handful and lean forward, letting the gems fall between my fingers, creating little waves in the otherwise smooth-as-glass liquid. My reflection is shadowed, nothing more than a halo of starlight around my face and head.

I don't know how long I've been here, but I think it's been long enough. Too long, I believe, to keep telling myself I'll wake up.

I miss everyone. I miss my father and Annabel the most. I miss Kael even though we've only met in our dreams. That doesn't feel like enough to me, but if the Goddess is the one protecting me now, trying to keep me sane while I linger in Morgathra's clutches, I hope She's also protecting him from the wicked witch's wrath.

A sharp echo of unidentifiable sound rushes toward me, making the pebbles tremble. I rise, turning to the source of the noise as another great door opens for me. I don't recognize this one, but I walk to it nonetheless, peeking into a den of darkness, of silent nothingness, before stepping into its embrace.

The darkness fades, replaced by a long, seemingly endless hallway of dark stone I don't find even remotely familiar. No doors line the walls, no windows, nor are there sconces to light my way. Just stone. Gray, slightly damp stone.

I turn back to the door, but instead of pulling the handle, my hand meets a flat, hard… wall. A shred of panic laces through my body as I go completely still. Voices drift toward me on a phantom breeze. Roars like thunder echo over the voices, making the floor beneath me tremble.

"What do you have to show me?" I ask out loud, my voice quivering as I keep my hand firmly planted against the wall.

I'm answered by voices again, but the words are jumbled, too quiet and quick to make out anything intelligible.

I turn my spine to steel and whirl away from the wall, walking on bare feet, following the noises that funnel into crashing, twisting music. But it's not music. The sounds crash and bang as I walk the length of the hallway, turning to something sinister, something so loud and violent it makes my ears ring. Unease creeps over my body like a million tiny spiders, my skin crawling, and I press myself against the wall, shielding my ears from the thunderous booms with my hands.

There're no doors. Not a single one. I look for a place to go, somewhere to find shelter from what I can only describe as the sounds of a great, horrifically bloody battle, but there's nowhere safe, nowhere quiet. The hallway continues, the far end a void of black, but that's where the noises are coming from, and I really don't want to go there.

Not at all.

"I want out," I cry, squeezing my eyes shut as another roar splits the air into pieces. "I'm done! Whatever this is, I don't want to see it!"

A rush of air fans over me—bright and warm. Outdoor air, I realize. I open my eyes expecting to find myself somewhere new, but I'm still here, in the hallway, trapped.

"Maxiana!" Kael shouts, and I stiffen.

"K-Kael? Kael?!" I shout, whirling toward his voice. The other voices are growing stronger, cutting through the sounds of battle. "KAEL!"

"Do you really think you stand a chance against someone like me?" sneers a female voice I find oddly familiar.

"Kael," I gasp breathlessly, dread burrowing into my bones. I leave the wall, racing down the hallway, ignoring the sound of flapping wings, of roars, of painful screeches that threaten to burst my eardrums.

A flash of green light burns my irises, and I stumble back, panting, and the hallway goes so impossibly quiet I can hear my own racing heartbeat.

For a few seconds, that's all there is. Silence. Then a slithering sound erupts all around me. Vines burst from the walls, the floor, racing down the hallway in my direction at an outrageous rate of speed. Like thick snakes, they slither and coil around my feet before I have a chance to react, and when one of them curls around my ankle, the pressure biting, I yelp, leaping away before its companions can pin me to the wall.

"KAEL!" I scream, racing toward the void. Vines explode through the wall, some as thin as my forearm while others are thicker than my thighs, and reach for me, trying to trip me, trying to catch my hair and pull me to a stop.

They lash against my legs, my arms, drawing blood. They snap and hiss like they're alive, and I risk a glance behind me, my lungs refusing to release air as a wall of vines careens in my direction, tendrils reaching and groping thin air.

I scream Kael's name again, tears burning my cheeks, but the hallway goes on, and on, and the vines are catching up to me.

One of the vines whips across the back of my legs like a knife. I fall to my knees, and the vines immediately wrap tight around my ankles, dragging me back.

I claw the ground, my fingernails raking over the flat, cold stone.

Kael calls out my name again, but it's faint. I scream for him, my skin splitting as the vines dig into my legs, crawling up my body. They lock my legs together, pulling and tugging. Several tendrils lace around my middle, and I'm... trapped.

A soft female voice echoes through the tunnel. Her words are unintelligible, a spell, I believe, that she whispers then shouts, her voice moving from calm to frantic, tuned to the beat of a drum.

The vines pin me to the ground belly down, reaching for my shoulders, dragging me closer and closer to the mass writhing only feet behind me.

"I'm so sorry," Kael's voice whispers as it washes through the air. "I came for you. I'm here. I tried. Maxiana–"

I reach for him, vines coiling around the length of my arm to the tips of my fingers. "My mate. *He's my mate*," I whisper, tears blurring my vision, and a vine coils around my neck.

I feel him all of the sudden, his presence all around me. His finger knit with mine, his scent overwhelming, his warmth shocking my body as the vines squeeze every inch of my skin.

A sharp pain erupts on my neck, and the vine trying to strangle me screeches in pain before letting go, but I'm drowning in them, squeezed so tight I haven't been able to breathe, and the already dark hallway is rapidly descending into shadows.

I'm pulled, ripped from the vines. My body slides across the ground, broken and bleeding, as I drag out a breath–my last.

Everything is silent for a long moment. Darkness embraces me. It's calming in a way. I almost give into it.

But then I'm thrust back into it for a moment. Memories of the vines explode in my mind, but this time, I'm warm and safe, being lifted into someone's arms. Kael's voice and the fading sounds of battle dissolve, replaced by the silence of the beach of gems.

Starlight shimmers overhead, blurring the face and shoulders of whoever's carrying me toward the water. I grip his shirt, my broken body limp in his arms. Water ripples around him as he walks for quite some time, and then he stops and turns, and I see the beach spread out—a beach of fallen stars.

"Are you ready?" Kael asks, his face cast in complete shadow.

I nod, and he takes one more step, and then we're swept into the water like we've fallen off a cliff, and the stars flicker black.

For a moment, there's nothing again. Nothing bleeds into gray, then silver darkness, as I open my eyes to a room I find faintly familiar. My arms are limp at my sides and useless. My eyes flutter, feeling heavy, like they've been closed for an eternity and aren't used to working any longer.

Moonlight drifts over a four poster bed lined with lace curtains that drift in a summer night breeze. The smell of blood is thick, and a soft pattering of what I believe might be water sounds to the left, in the corner of a snug room of stone.

The room groans around me. Crumbling, falling stone echoes through my ears, but then I regain sense of my body, and feel someone warm pressing their face into the crook of my shoulder, his mouth pressed to my neck as his body trembles, his arms wrapped tight around my back.

A dragon's roar pierces the silence in the room, and my body jolts, rebelling against the sharp, echoing sound.

The man lifts his head, looking down at me. His eyes are dark—nearly black—but flaked with blues and golden, like stars. He's devastatingly handsome, his features sharp and regal. He's… beautiful, like he was carved by an old god. Moonlight drifts across his cheekbones, illuminating the powerful, glimmery scales barely visible beneath his skin.

I weakly grip his arm, dragging in a ragged breath, filling my lungs with air—real air.

"Kael," I croak, trying to breathe again, finding it hard, like a weight has been pressed to my chest for an achingly long period of time.

"Max," he breathes, my name leaving his lips like he can't believe it.

"I—" My fingers twitch as feeling starts to whisper through my body again, tingling sharply as blood rushes. I weakly lift my arm, hesitating before running my fingertips over his cheek while he stares down at me in disbelief. "Is this real? Or another dream?"

He leans into the touch when I caress his cheek, drinking in his warmth while my fingers tingle. He turns over my hand, pressing a soft kiss to my palm. But then his eyes widen, and he looks down at me, his jaw tightening, muscles ticking then flexing.

"It's real," he says gravely, then turns his face to the vine-covered windows as a screech rattles the castle, followed by the boom of dragon roars.

The room comes into view, but I don't have a second to take it in. He scoops me into his arms and stands, whirling like he's looking for something. He clutches me to his chest, cradling me like I weigh nothing, and snatches something off the ground. Metal sings as a sword slices across the floor tiles, and then I see… blood.

So much blood.

A man is in pieces nearby, what's left of his body slumped against the wall, his eyes open but unseeing.

I gasp, but Kael is already turning me away from the horrible scene, and then we're plunged into darkness again when he walks through a doorway, racing down stairs covered in writhing vines.

But they don't reach for us. In fact, they shake, uncoiling themselves from each other, hissing and trembling in what seems like pain. I find the strength to lift my head, watching them as Kael rushes down a spiral staircase enclosed in dark stone.

He reaches another door and steps out into a familiar corridor. We're in my castle, my home in Vaeloria.

"My father," I rush out. I grip Kael's shirt until my knuckles turn white.

"I'll find him, I swear," he says, but his attention is on something else. He tilts his head, closing his eyes for a moment, wincing like he's hurt, but when he opens his eyes again, several booming roars shake the ceiling height windows overlooking the vine covered front garden, and a looming, black shadow appears.

Kael keeps his eyes on the massive shadow as he turns, racing over vines toward the grand foyer. Vines are everywhere, covering every surface, covering what I realize are bodies... bodies dressed for my ball.

Fear ties a knot in my chest so tight I can't breathe, can't form the words I need to ask what happened and how much time passed.

But then cool night air dusts over my cheeks. Another man appears, jogging toward Kael, his eyes cast in shadow and body covered in scale-like armor.

"Ryker," Kael says sharply, cutting the man's questions off before he can even begin, "take her to the woods. Guard her with your life."

The man stares at me, and I stare back, unsure what to think of this rough, frightening looking... dragon.

Kael thrusts me into Ryker's arms.

"Kael!" I screech, reaching for him.

But he takes several steps away, then his body erupts in a veil of shimmering, black mist, and my mate...

Is transformed.

SOMETHING MORE

MAXIANA

I HAVE TWO SECONDS TO CATCH MY BREATH, TO UNRAVEL AND DIGEST what I'm seeing, before Kael lifts his massive, jet-black wings and soars into the night sky, his roar sending a shockwave that nearly knocks me to the ground. His man, Ryker, catches me by the arm and tugs me close as I watch the shadow of my mate soar against the moonlight, joining a league of dragons fighting to what seems like the death against their own kind.

"What's happening?" I blurt out, finding it hard to stay upright. My legs feel like jelly, and my mind isn't in much better shape.

"War," Ryker says simply, quietly, then tugs me toward the garden where the roping, tangled vines are starting to fall in on themselves, slowly turning to ash. A warm wind driven by dragon wings whips across my cheeks, my hair billowing down my back. I'm wearing the shift I wore under the gown from the ball, and I'm barefoot, dressed exactly like I was when I was trapped in the dreamworld.

But this is real. Too real. Rocks bite into my feet as Ryker guides me backward, looking for a clean exit from the gnarled garden.

Everything is washed in gray. What was once a beautiful rose garden is now flattened, spring blooms decaying and crumpled under the weight of the wines. Many of the buildings that once hugged the garden wall are falling in on themselves, and the wall itself is shattered, unable to withstand the weight of Morgathra's magic.

Horror rushes through me, twisting into despair. "My people. My pack. Where are they? Where is everyone?" My voice strains against the words. "My father?"

More dragons soar overhead, tumbling through the sky together. Ryker continues to tug me out of the garden, unable to answer my question, but my eyes are on the sky as I watch the black dragon–my dragon–pierces the thunderclouds moving swiftly over the city. A startlingly silver dragon meets him as he dives, the two of them splitting a faction of enemy dragons into pieces. Their roars sing through the air, sending a chill up my spine.

"Come, Princess. We need to hurry."

"Where are we going?"

I follow Ryker out of the garden and around the side of the castle. My bare feet are cut and aching, but the vines continue to dissolve, puffs of gray ash filling the air as I race after Ryker, his hand still firmly curled around my wrist.

He helps me over the wall around the castle ground, catching me by the waist. The woods beyond are dark and all consuming, sucking the moonlight from the sky before it can even touch the ground.

He curses under his breath when I trip over my own feet. He scoops me into his arms and begins to sprint, racing through the trees. I steal a look over his shoulder as the woods swallow us. The castle falls away, and the roars and pained cries of the dragons fade, but Ryker keeps running.

"Where are we–"

"Kael commanded me to take you to the plains just beyond Vaeloria, just beyond this stretch of woods," he pants, wincing as he leaps over a felled tree. "We're nearly there. We have a camp there."

"Why aren't we flying?" I ask, my voice trembling as I'm jostled like a rag doll, gripping the smooth, scaled surface of what I can only describe as armor that covers his entire body.

"I'm hurt. My right wing–" He leaps again, landing with a crunch, but keeps running as the trees start to thin, and the plains open up, firelight dancing only a quarter mile away but...

Blood scents the air. Thick, like molten iron. I have a single second to suck in a breath and scream before green-hued light blinds us both. Ryker falls to his knees, and I roll out of his arms.

Keening female cries cut through the distant roar of the dragons–closer to us, gaining on us.

Ryker is on his feet again in an instant, yanking me upright, but another rush of green light rolls toward us through the woods.

"We need to go, now!" he shouts, grabbing my arm and pulling me in the direction of the plains. The green light cuts out just feet away, but that smell... blood. Metallic and heavy. It stains the inside of my nose as I choke back the taste and turn with him, rushing toward the firelight, praying we're moving fast enough. Another gust of light rips through the forest, and Ryker gets caught like he's just fallen into a snare.

I scream, tumbling back to the ground hard, his body breaking my fall. He grunts in pain when I collide with him, the two of his rolling down a short, but steep, decline. Another gust of green light soars just a foot above my head. I curl my body over Ryker's, shielding him from the spray of what I now know is magic, and hold us to the ground.

Dragon wings beat the air overhead, making the trees bow and tremble. Screeches fill the forest as heat like I've never experienced before singes my back, and light fills my vision–firelight.

"Stay low!" Ryker shouts, grabbing me around the waist and pulling me underneath him, covering me with his body instead of the other way around. Another burst of fire scorches the forest, and Ryker braces himself, his elbows bent to stop from crushing me, as trees begin to snap and fall over us.

"Are those your dragons?" I bellow, hoping he can hear me over the chaos.

"Maybe," he admits, panting.

Smoke fills the air and a battle between fire and light rages around us. The ground begins to heat, and it's unbearable. Ryker seems unfazed, but it must be his scales protecting his skin. I'm having trouble catching my breath.

He notices, lifts his head, and grunts with effort as he lifts me from the ground and starts running away.

For a moment, I feel like I'm just drifting. Fire rages overhead, the sky full of smoke that erupts in eerie shades of green as witches battle dragons.

"This is because of me," I whisper over the fray knowing Ryker can't hear me, but it doesn't matter. My vision starts going dark–too dark–the kind of darkness I languished in for far too long.

I don't want to go back there.

Ryker breaches the trees. Shouts in the distance fill my ears. He seems to relax, though he's still breathing hard, while I keep my eyes on the smoky sky, the full moon now completely consumed.

"SHIFT!" someone shouts. "COMMANDER RYKER! BEHIND YOU! SHIFT!"

"I CAN'T!" Ryker bellows. "I'M WOUNDED AND IF I SHIFT, I'LL CRUSH HER!"

A silver flash breaks through the smoke as the sky turns green again, followed by a black shadow, much closer this time, diving toward us.

I feel the magic. My skin prickles in warning as a rush of green light explodes over us, around us.

Kael dives a moment too late.

Ryker rolls to the ground, narrowly missing the surge of green light. I hit the forest floor with a crunch as the magic consumes Kael, dragging him out of the sky.

He's silent as he falls, tumbling, and meets the earth with a shattering crack that makes the ground roll and tremble for several seconds.

"No," I say, my voice cracking painfully, my throat scorched from the smoke. "No–"

Ryker groans before going still.

I reach to the side, gripping grass between my fingers. My head spins as the smoke descends, the green light spiraling all around us.

I think of my father–a kind, somewhat oblivious man. He didn't know what my mother was. He didn't understand. All he wanted to do was help her, save her, save me.

He loved me wholly, truly, and utterly. I was his world. I know now that he knew about the curse. He spent twenty-one years in purgatory, counting down the years, the days, the hours, the minutes until my birthday, wondering if I'd survive.

He could be dead now.

More green light fills my vision. Deep in my chest, a sharp pain radiates, followed by several painful plucking sensations that steal what little breath I have to spare.

I think about Annabel, my only friend. Is she at the castle? Is she dead, too?

More pain fills my chest, my heart caving in on itself.

I think of my mother–a woman I never knew. A woman hunted and hidden, protected by her mate. A woman who found the truest kind of love for a few sweet years before she was taken from us.

A searing sensation explodes through my chest, ripping me to shreds from the inside.

I think of Kael. My mate. My dragon mate. The man who went to war to save me–and is… is dying.

My scream can be heard in the heavens as the final strings binding me to him break free, and he slips away.

I barely register sound and feeling as I rise to my knees, my scream of agony silent, my jaw straining as my chest drains of air.

All around me, dragons fall from the sky, trapped in a haze of smoke and magic, unable to stay airborne. The silver dragon careens to the ground out of control but shifts into a man before he touches down, his body breaking, then going still.

This isn't right. Something about this isn't right. The curse—I broke the curse, didn't I? I survived. Kael brought me back.

I rise, turning to the source of the magic, a woman standing alone, battered, at the edge of the forest, barely able to stand as she sends her powers into the air, cutting through the dragons still fighting for control.

Kael fell between us. He's in his human form now, flat on his back, motionless, his eyes open as he stares sightless at the sky.

I raise my hands as something new whispers through my body. A change deep in the marrow of my bones. Something ingrained deep in my soul—something that makes me who I am—a shifter, but that's not all. I'm also something else.

Something more.

My body breaks, curling in on itself, tumbling into something new and made of raw power. Light whispers from my body as skin turns to fur, as my hands and feet turn to paws.

On the full moon, a month after my birthday, I shift for the first time.

I'm golden, just like my mother was.

Light pours from my fur, illuminating the smoke, cutting through the haze of green and black.

Morgathra, fighting her last stand as her curse shatters around her, sends her magic toward me in a beam of green, dark power.

I race into it, splitting it into pieces, my golden light cutting through her power like butter.

I don't think. I don't feel. I just act, my paws pounding the ground as I race toward my mate, my power leaving a trail of gold in my wake that soaks into the ground, fanning out across the plains.

Morgathra screams, but I cut it short, leaping off my paws and colliding with the witch, my jaw wide and my perfect, sharpened teeth gleaming as I clamp down on her neck and roll, tearing her head from her body.

Screams of agony and fear fill the forest before tapering out in ribbons of pain.

The coven of darkness dies in an instant, every witch tethered to Morgathra's power, her promise, wiped out in a single blow.

The green light shutters before dissolving into smoke, and the forest goes quiet, nothing but crackling embers to fill the void of silence.

My wolf powers shudder. I rise, stretching out of my wolf and back into my aching, exhausted human body, but the golden light remains, and my glow is… immense.

I raise my hands toward the field, toward the fallen dragons, and send my light as far as I can, and it takes all of the strength I have.

For several seconds, there's nothing but light, like the sun has risen again, beating the smoke into submission.

And then it ends, whispering away, clearing the smoke until the moon and stars are visible once more.

I fall to my knees beside Kael as my vision goes black, and feel my cheek hit his chest when I let the darkness consume me, praying wherever I'm going next I'm at least with him.

AFTER A LONG SLEEP

Kael

"Kael–Kael! Wake up!" Ashton's voice rings through my ears, and then I'm being yanked by the shoulders into a sitting position before I even open my eyes. Cool night air funnels around me, igniting my senses, and I choke on the first breath I take like I haven't filled my lungs in ages.

I smell smoke. Heavy smoke, like a fire rages nearby, but the sky is shockingly clear, the moon full and bright against a backdrop of stars, but…

Ashton fills my vision, his silver armor matching those of his men, some of which are still in dragon forms scattered around the plains near the wall that encloses Vaeloria.

"What–" I breathe, unsure what I'm seeing. "Why aren't we still in the sky? What happened?"

Ashton, wild eyed, shakes his head, unable to answer.

"Ashton?"

I see her then, her golden hair catching the light of the moon. She's lying a few feet away, her back to me, her nightgown shredded and barely covering her skin. I move before my mind has a chance to catch up, crawling over what I realize is scorched earth, to my mate's side. I roll her onto her back, smoothing my hand over her cheek. "Maxiana, you have to wake up."

Her eyes are closed tight.

"Max," I press, shaking her by the shoulders. "Come on. You need to wake–wake up! WAKE UP!"

"Kael–" Ashton tries to squeeze my shoulder, but I shrug him off.

I rise, lifting Maxiana into my arms, and turn to the dragons and warriors stumbling around the clearing, their eyes narrowed against the smoke I realize is funneling from the forest where a fire of epic proportions once raged but is now reduced to smoldering embers.

Dragon fire scents the air, tinged with something else–something rancid and heady. Magic, I realize, as I scan the field.

Vaeloria is only five-hundred or so yards away, its boundary wall in shambles, but what was once a pile of twisting vines is now ash that lifts in the soft breeze drifting through forest on all sides.

It all comes back to me. The battle in the skies with King Titus's men, who had no idea he was dead. The green light as Morgathra made her last stand as her curse broke, and she had nothing left to lose.

I remember seeing Ryker below trying to get back to where our men were stationed, using this clearing, this two mile long strip of grass leading up to Vaeloria, as a landing pad, a place to rest, but… he was struggling against the magic coming from the forest, and Maxiana was with him.

That moment of distraction… I shouldn't be alive. I remember diving for them, desperate, flying straight into the magic that was pulling my men, and Ashton's men, to their deaths, causing us to shift back to our human forms mid-flight, unable to stop the fall.

Buildings in Vaeloria are crumbling as the vines fall away, and bricks and stone falling to the ground in the distance is the only sound for several seconds.

"Is it over?" Ryker asks nearby, panting, looking down at his hands like he can't believe he's alive.

But Ashton is still hovering, looking nervously down at the limp woman in my arms.

"That's her, isn't it? Princess Maxiana—"

"She's my mate," I growl. There's no way around it, no reason to beat around the bush. I can feel her heartbeat quaking, so faint I nearly miss it.

"Do you know what she's done?" Ashton whispers, and I look up at him, confused and unsure about the look of disbelief washing over his features.

He doesn't have a scratch on him. Not a single bruise, nor open wound. In fact, all of the men and dragons in the clearing are... flawless, like they haven't just been through hell and back.

I look down at her, at the color beginning to fill back into her cheeks, and close my eyes.

The golden light. I remember now. The dream I had of her when I was injured and in Queen Maeve's care—that had been her, hadn't it?

This little shifter woman—this wolf—possesses the gift of healing. There used to be a type of dragon with that gift—a coveted breed that's no longer in existence.

Somewhere down her line, her mother was passed a single drop of dragon's blood, enough to pass on this gift of healing, this gift of light that saved my life, and everyone else's.

I cradle Max in my arms as shouts ring out in the distance. Several of my men startle when shadows start appearing at the boundary wall.

Villagers. The townspeople in Vaeloria waking up from their stupor are now filling the streets, confused and fearful.

"Ashton, take your men into the sky and canvas the woods for any signs of Morgathra's coven. Make sure they're dead." I turn to Ryker. "We need to head back into the town, provide aid."

"Is she going to be all right?" Ryker asks with great effort. "Annabel—I swore to her she'd see Maxiana again."

"She'll be okay," I say, even if I'm not sure. Everything that's happening feels like we're still stuck in that dreamworld, even when she's whole and warm in my arms.

I start moving toward the wall when the shouts reach a peak. My men move in swiftly, telling the villagers to stay out of the streets and away from crumbling buildings, but there's nowhere they can go that's truly untouched. Devastation is everywhere–fire burns the enchanted forest, ash covers every surface, and glass is scattered as far as the eye can see when I step over the wall and walk into the street with Maxiana still in my arms, holding her tight.

Confused townspeople watch me carrying their princess, their jaws ajar.

There's one place she'll want to be when she wakes up.

Home.

It's nearly silent when I walk back into the castle. A few of my men follow to help direct the ball-goers, who succumbed to the curse a month ago, somewhere safe, but I carry my mate into the ballroom, into the party she never had a chance to attend. I walk the same path I took when I first came here, unsure what to expect, not knowing what I signed up for, not understanding the pull I felt toward the princess locked away in that tower.

Her father still lies near his throne, covered in ash from head to toe.

Maxiana turns her head with a groan.

"You're okay," I whisper, lowering her to the ground. I pull what I believe is a cape off the floor and wrap it around her shoulders, sitting her upright, letting her breathe and blink to wake herself up. She opens those gorgeous eyes to the ballroom and startles, then calms, her eyes slowly meeting mine again.

"We won," I tell her, kneeling on the steps in front of her so we're eye to eye. "You broke the curse, Maxiana."

She reaches out, caresses my cheek. "You broke the curse. You saved me."

"You led me here in your dreams. It was you this entire time. I've been dreaming of you for years now, not knowing where you were or where I could find you."

"I have been dreaming of you, too," she admits with the softest, most beautiful smile.

I kiss her, and my body ignites, but then her father groans, and her attention snaps to him.

"Father?" Max asks, reaching for him, but she's weak. Her fingers tremble as she touches his face, then pulls back when he sucks in a breath.

I remain where I am but grip her shoulder to keep her steady as she lifts a hand, noticing her father is struggling to wake up, to get out from under the yoke of the remnants of the curse. I watch in awe as her fingers begin to glow a soft gold against the darkness in the room, and she places her hand on his chest, bowing her head and letting that light fill him.

She rocks forward, trembling against the surge of her powers, but I hold her steady, saying, "That's enough. You've done enough."

"We've gathered the villagers in the town square," Ryker shouts from the other end of the room. Now, my men are moving into the ballroom, gathering startled guests who likely fell asleep and didn't know they were buried under piles of vines, cursed along with every other person in this town.

Max's light flickers out when I tell Ryker, "Find whatever buildings are structurally safe. Send men back to Starfall for supplies. We'll need tents, anything you can get your hands on. We'll rebuild this city, that's a promise."

"Maxiana," The Alpha King of Ebonclaw whispers with effort, finally opening his eyes.

I feel like I can breathe again, and rise, leaving the two of them alone for a moment but not straying far. I keep an eye on her as I reach Ryker's side, saying, "Send two scouts to Hexeton with a message for Queen Maeve. Vaeloria didn't fall, but the people need help. She has a duty to them as the queen of the witches. Ask for her healers. She'll send them."

"Are you sure she will?"

"She will," I tell him because otherwise she'll have to deal with me again, and I don't plan on being as nice as I was the last time around.

I turn back to Maxiana and catch the moment her father realizes the curse has been broken. He weeps, sitting up and embracing his daughter.

I feel a sudden jolt of unease watching them, knowing what comes next.

She's my mate. That is so impossibly rare. But I… I would let her go if that's what she wants, if being here is what she needs.

She turns to look at me, giving me the saddest smile, and my heart shatters.

"Go to her. We've got everything else covered," Ryker says, clapping my shoulder.

I nod, moving away from the other dragons clearing out the ballroom.

"You. I remember you," the king whispers when I come into sight.

"Father," Maxiana smiles, tears in her eyes. "This is Kael."

"King of the Dragons," he says under his breath, but his eyes slide from me to Maxiana.

She gives him a weak smile. "He's my mate. I found my mate, Father."

Now he's looking at me again. I turn my spine to steel, bowing my head in a brief show of submission to the father of my mate, waiting for the worst.

But when I straighten, he's smiling, tears in his eyes.

"We'll hold another ball," he says, his cheeks turning rosy as he smiles. "To celebrate the match. What a blessing this is, my daughter. A mate. You've found him. Now you know the happiness I knew with your mother."

Maxiana bursts into tears, and I can't take it any longer.

"Take her to her room," the king says. "Put her to bed. I have to check on my pack."

A ROYAL WEDDING

Maxiana

"The gown is made of moonlight," Annabel whispers when she lifts it from the velvet-lined chest, and I believe her.

It was my mother Aurora's wedding gown, and the fabric gleams silver and pearl in the morning sun, sheer as breath, yet heavy with enchantment. Diamond-laced embroidery shimmers across the bodice like frost on glass, and the hem is edged in sapphire thread that looks as though it was spun from the stars themselves.

Annabel hums as she works on my hair, her hands deft as always, weaving strands into an intricate crown of braids.

"You'll take his breath, my lady," she says, voice soft. "King Kael won't remember his own name when he sees you."

My lips curve. "He better remember mine."

She giggles, the sound bright.

Light spills through the stained-glass windows, casting halos of ruby and emerald across the marble floor. I touch my fingertip, still faintly marked where I pricked it on that cursed thorn, Morgathra's cruel spell.

And Kael rescued me.

"Lift your arms, my lady," Annabel murmurs, holding the gown before me.

I slip into it, and it molds to my body like magic, the bodice tightening around my waist and the skirts flaring out into oceans of glistening fabric.

I see my reflection in the mirror. My collarbone is dusted in shimmery powder, my eyelids dabbed silvery-blue, and my lips painted wine red.

The necklace Kael sent lies nestled in a box of ivory silk. I lift it carefully. A single teardrop emerald hangs from a chain of braided gold. Annabel fastens it around my neck and steps back, tears shining in her eyes. "They will sing of this day for centuries."

She exhales when she finishes and steps back, clasping her hands together.

"There," she breathes. "You are ready, my lady."

But I don't feel ready. My pulse is too loud. My throat is dry, though I've been sipping blackberry wine. My hands tremble, and not from fear, but from the sheer magnitude of it all.

Today, I become Kael's wife.

Today I become Queen.

I smooth the fabric over my hips and glance at the mirror once more just as we hear a knock on the chamber door. Three slow, deliberate taps.

Annabel turns to open it and dips into a curtsey.

Standing in the doorway is my father. He wears his ceremonial armor—not the full weight of it, but the polished breastplate and bracers that catch the light with every movement. A deep violet cloak edged in silver thread, drapes from his broad shoulders. His face, usually so stern and unyielding, is softened by emotion, and his eyes shimmer with unshed tears.

"Maxiana," he says, voice low and steady. "Are you ready, daughter?"

I nod.

He crosses the chamber in measured strides then offers me his arm without a word of doubt. His voice is low, reverent. "Your mother would have wept tears of joy to see you like this. So radiant, and fiercely beautiful.

The corridor is quiet, lit with lanterns that cast a glow on the polished marble floor. My father walks beside me, his arm steady beneath my hand, his ceremonial cloak brushing the ground.

"You've grown into everything your mother hoped for," he says, his voice thick with emotion.

"I never imagined happiness could feel this full of life," I whisper. "Kael is everything I didn't know I needed."

I glance back at Annabel following us in silence, her hands folded, a smile on her lips.

Standing at the threshold of the grand crystal hall, the weight of my gown pooling behind me, Annabel presses a kiss to my cheek, and I squeeze her hand before stepping forward.

Father stands beside me, tall and regal in his formal armor, the violet cloak billowing behind him like twilight smoke. He offers his arm, and I take it, grounding myself in the familiar strength of his presence. His hand trembles just slightly, though his jaw is set in that stoic way it always is when he's hiding emotion. I glance up at him and find his eyes glistening again. He doesn't speak, but he doesn't have to. He's giving me away—not because I'm his to give, but because this is a day we never thought would come.

The aisle stretches ahead, a gleaming ribbon of white marble streaked with gold, glowing softly beneath the chandeliers. Red and white rose petals lie scattered like a royal offering, their delicate fragrance rising with each step we take. On either side of the aisle, nobles and guests rise.

At the aisle's end, beneath a grand canopy shimmering with softly glowing lanterns, stands the man I've loved long before I knew his name. His face is sharp and noble, with a strength that commands the room and a softness reserved only for me. His robes of rich emerald and onyx are embroidered with threads of gold that catch the light with every movement. A crown of gold and obsidian rests on his brow, accented by an emerald the size of a plum—glowing quietly, seemingly alive with light.

Moon Goddess help me. He's looking at me now like I'm the only woman in the universe.

My throat tightens with nervous excitement as we reach the end, and Father places my hand into Kael's. The moment his fingers touch mine, the mark of our bond glows faintly across my palm—a sigil of fire entwined with a wolf's fang, born of blood and magic.

"Max," Kael whispers, his voice rich and low and only for me. "You're breathtaking."

"Thank you. You are so handsome," I say, my voice shaking with joy.

He smiles, and the room fades away.

The officiant begins to speak, her voice like chimes through the high-arched hall. Ancient vows, sacred oaths, the blessings of both moon and flame. As she speaks, Kael and I turn to each other. He lifts my hands and kisses each one. I feel the burn of happy tears behind my eyes.

"I pledge my soul to yours," he says, his voice steady and sure. "In shadow and in light. In fire, in ice, in peace, and in war. My heart is yours, forever."

I repeat the vow, only my voice isn't as steady.

He places the ring upon my finger—a band of white gold, shaped like a twisting flame and set with a teardrop-shaped opal-hued moonstone. I slide his onto his finger—wolf steel, bound with emerald.

The officiant steps back.

"You may shift," she says.

Gasps ripple through the crowd. My skin warms. Kael's eyes shimmer green.

I step behind the velvet curtain, trembling with excitement as Annabel unlaces the back of my mother's gown. The fabric falls off my shoulders like a memory, pooling at my feet.

I close my eyes and shift. Bone, breath, fur and strength, my wolf bursts free, fierce and radiant.

Kael is already waiting, his dragon wreathed in fire. And I am my golden wolf, sleek and glowing under the lantern light. For one perfect moment, flame and fur, tooth and scale, we touch, a new bond flashing between us, ancient and unbreakable.

And then, hand in hand, man and woman once more, we turn to face our people.

A roar erupts—cheers, music, the thunder of feet on stone.

We are one.

The grand hall is alive with light and sound. Crystal chandeliers hang from towering ceilings, scattering prisms of color that dance across tapestries woven with threads of gold and silver. The scent of jasmine and amber fills the air, mingling with the rich aromas of spiced meats, fresh fruits, and sweet pastries. It's as if the castle itself is celebrating with us, breathing warmth and life into every corner.

Guests from across both our kingdoms, nobles and shifters alike, swirl through the hall in gowns and robes that gleam with jewels—rubies that catch the firelight like captured flames, sapphires deep as midnight seas, and diamonds that sparkle like frozen stars. The music swells, a lilting melody played on harp and lyre, blending with the rhythmic pulse of drums that speak of ancient rites and new beginnings.

I glide beside Kael, feeling the weight of his hand steady on my waist, the strength of his presence grounding me. His emerald robes shimmer beneath the soft light, the golden embroidery catching my eye every time he moves. Around us, the murmurs of admiration follow—he's the Dragon King, fierce and revered; I am the witch wolf shifter princess born of fire and shadow, bound to him by blood and fate.

I catch sight of Annabel and Ryker near the edge of the dance floor, talking quietly. She's smiling in that soft, surprised way she does when someone catches her off guard, and Ryker, usually all sharp edges and silence, actually laughs.

The feast begins. Long tables groan under the weight of delicacies: roasted pheasant glazed with honey and herbs, platters of fresh river trout sprinkled with crushed emerald salt, baskets overflowing with berries kissed by cream. Goblets clink as toasts rise in waves.

Kael leans close to me, his breath warm against my ear. "You shine brighter than all the jewels tonight," he murmurs. I press a hand to his chest, feeling the steady beat of his heart beneath the royal robes.

We rise to make our first toast as mates, voices ringing clear across the hall. "To the future," Kael says, his eyes never leaving mine. "To fire and shadow intertwined. To love fierce enough to change the world."

Cheers erupt, a thunderous wave of celebration. The music quickens, drums beating faster as dancers take to the floor. Silken skirts swirl, and boots beat rhythms on the stone.

Time melts away. Laughter spills like warm honey; stories are told in whispered tones and booming laughs. The king's court brings gifts —an exquisite necklace of jade and amethyst for me, a silver blade forged with dragon fire for Kael. Each gift is a promise, a blessing, a thread woven into the fabric of our new life.

I steal a moment with Kael on a balcony, the stars above alive, twinkling like diamonds scattered across velvet.

He brushes a stray curl from my face. "You are safe now. I will always protect you."

"You will always have my gratitude and you will always have my heart," I reply.

I lean back into his chest, and he wraps his arms around me, the truth of our vows settling deep in my bones. The path ahead won't be easy. There are threats lurking, enemies who would see us torn apart, but tonight is ours. Tonight, we are whole.

Returning to the hall, the night deepens but the energy never wanes. Music swells again, voices raised in joyous song. I catch the proud smile of my father watching from his seat.

As dawn approaches, the crowd begins to thin, but the warmth remains. Kael and I stand together, hands entwined, surrounded by friends, family, and allies. The future is uncertain, but for the first time, I feel ready—because I am not alone.

HONEYMOON HEAVEN

Maxiana

The doors to our bedchamber close behind us with a soft thud. The air here is warmer, heavy with the scent of lavender and the subtle burn of dragon fire incense. Soft tapestries of deep greens and golds drape the walls, shimmering like liquid flame beneath the flicker of candlelight.

Kael stands close, his gaze dark and steady, holding me in the quiet gravity of the moment. There's no need for words; everything between us hums with the promise of what's to come. My pulse quickens beneath his touch, a steady thrum that matches the rhythm of his breath.

His fingers trace the curve of my jaw, rough against my skin in a way that makes me shiver. "You are mine," he says, low and sure, the raw strength in his voice wrapping around me like a cloak.

I nod, unable to speak, caught in the pull of his presence. My hands find the edges of his robe, sliding over the smooth fabric, burning beneath my fingertips.

Slowly, Kael lowers his mouth to mine. The kiss is slow to bloom, deep and searing, a dance of tongues and breath that melts away every sorrow I've ever carried. His lips are both gentle and demanding, claiming and worshipping, as if this moment is the culmination of every lifetime we've shared.

His hands roam my back, the strength there steady and certain, grounding me even as my heart races with desperate need. The silk of my gown slips between my fingers, and with a quiet, urgent grace, he peels it away. The cool air brushes my skin, making the heat between us flare even brighter.

I reach up, fingertips sliding beneath his collar tracing the sculpted planes of his shoulders. His skin is warm and solid, the muscles beneath taut and alive. My heart pounds as I press closer, craving the connection—the fierce, unbreakable bond that only he can give.

His hands move lower, mapping the curves of my waist, the swell of my hips, igniting a trail of fire wherever they touch. The lust within me thrums, wild and untamed, responding to his touch with a hunger I never knew I had.

His lips find my neck, trailing fire and shadow in equal measure, and I arch into him, surrendering to the exquisite torment of desire.

Kael lifts me into his arms and carries me to the bed. He doesn't rush, and his touch is careful. When we reach it, he lays me down gently.

He stands for a moment, watching me, then slowly undresses—shrugging off his clothing, unfastening each piece until there's nothing left between us.

Then he leans over me and peels my undergarments off, leaving behind nothing but my bare skin, radiating with lust.

Kael's lips and tongue find my nipples, tracing circles around them before kissing one and then the other. I run my fingers through his hair as he devours me with his mouth.

He draws soft, aching moans from me as his fingers find where I'm already wanting. I've never felt more alive—never felt more desired.

Kael finds the places that make me gasp, the ones that make my body arch toward his. At the same time, his mouth lingers on my breasts—kissing, tasting, drawing soft whimpers from deep in my throat. The combination unravels me. I lose all sense of time, of place —there's only Kael.

My breath catches as his fingers move with confidence, circling and pressing in just the right way. His mouth never leaves my breasts, his lips and tongue teasing, worshipping, while his hand works lower, deeper, until I can't think—can't breathe. The pressure builds, sharp and hot and dizzying. My hands clutch the sheets, my hips rising to meet every slow stroke, every flick of his tongue.

"Kael," I gasp, voice breaking. "I—"

He doesn't stop. He knows exactly what I need, and he gives it to me.

The world shatters.

I cry out, trembling beneath him, every nerve alight, every inch of me unraveling in waves of pleasure. My eyes squeeze shut as the climax crashes over me, and I feel him there, holding me through it— his mouth still pressed to my breast, his hand slowing only when I'm finally breathless and still.

I'm still catching my breath, my skin tingling where his mouth last touched me, when he moves over me. His body hovers just above mine, his eyes searching my face.

Kael guides himself into me, slow and careful at first, and when he enters, I gasp.

It's deeper, fuller, more intense than I imagined—like everything that's ever been missing is suddenly here, inside me. I clutch at his shoulders, drawing him closer, and he groans low in his throat, the sound raw and reverent.

We move together, finding a rhythm that's both tender and urgent, as if our bodies have always known each other. His mouth finds mine again—less like a kiss, more like a vow—and I melt beneath him, every nerve alight.

Pleasure builds again, faster this time, sharp and bright and over- whelming. I feel it rise in him too, in the way his breath catches, in the tension coiling through his body.

When at last we collapse together, spent and sated, the firelight flickers over our entwined forms, painting us in shadows. Kael's fingers thread through my hair as I rest my head against his chest, feeling the steady beat of his heart beneath my ear.

"I am yours," I whisper, voice raw and full of truth.

"And I am yours," he replies, his voice a fierce, gentle promise that settles deep in my soul.

A LEGACY

Kael

Two Months later.

The vines that once strangled Vaeloria's great hall have finally been cleared away. Light streams through high windows, catching on the stone floor.

Max stands at my side, her hand warm in mine, the silver cloak draped from her shoulders catching the light as it trails behind her. Her golden hair is pinned with Moonstones, and a soft flush touches her cheeks. Even in stillness, there's a wildness in her; an untamed strength just beneath the surface. She's radiant. Fierce. And she's mine.

Max's father steps forward, dressed in ceremonial robes, and the weight of his presence fills the room. Experience and tribulations have only sharpened him. Broad-shouldered and clear-eyed, his voice is steady as he turns to face the elders gathered around the long table.

"We have agreed," he says, nodding once toward Max and me. "My daughter and King Kael of the Emerald Coast are joined now in truth. Her place is by his side, ruling his lands and his people. And my place remains here, guiding the Ebonclaw pack until my time is done."

A murmur passes through the room. Looks of approval, relief, maybe even something close to joy wash over their faces.

The council has seen wars, famines, and evil spells. They lived through Vaeloria's decay under Morgathra's spell, vines crawling through stone and soil, twisting the land into something unrecognizable. But now, with the curse broken, they're ready for something more. Something alive and awake.

Max lifts her chin. "Vaeloria will not be forgotten. We'll send builders and masons to help rebuild the city, not just for the pack, but for every creature who calls this land home." She glances at me, and I squeeze her hand. "Emerald Coast will help. Our bond means restoration, unity, and love."

"It means peace," I add. "Our skies are free now, and your forests are waking. We've each endured our own darkness. It's time we share the light."

Max's father gives a short nod. "When I pass, the lands of Vaeloria and the rule of Ebonclaw will fall to Ryker and Annabel."

A glimmer of surprise moves through the room.

Max smiles. "We assure you, they'll be ready."

I turn toward the elders. "You are right to trust Ryker with this land, and with your people. He's loyal and will be a strong leader. He is my first in command, and I trained him myself."

"And Annabel," Max adds, "the people already love her. They'll follow her. She has the heart of a Luna."

The council of elders nods in solemn agreement, their weathered faces betraying a rare sense of unity. One by one, they rise and place their right fists over their hearts—a gesture of approval older than any crown.

The eldest among them steps forward and says, "The bond between wolf and dragon is rare, but the strength we see before us is undeniable. Let it be known: Kael of Starfall and Maxiana of Ebonclaw shall reign over the Emerald Coast, and our Alpha King shall continue to lead Vaeloria. When his time comes, the stewardship of this land will pass to Ryker and Annabel, with the full blessing of this council."

As the meeting begins to break apart, I feel Max lean lightly against me. She's quiet for a moment, her gaze sweeping across the old hall.

"It still feels like a dream," she says softly. "To stand here, free, married, and alive."

"You're not dreaming," I murmur. "You're mine, and I'm yours. We'll build something that lasts. Something no curse can touch."

She turns her face to me. "Two kingdoms."

"Bound by one flame," I say.

She laughs, low and beautiful, and for a moment I forget we're standing before ancient power and watching eyes. All I see is her. My wolf. My queen.

Together, we step forward into the hall as equals—Dragon King and Alpha-born. The curse broken, the kingdoms breathing again.

Ryker is still out on the training field, just past the outer wall. He doesn't miss a day. Even now, with no active war, no threat on our borders, he leads drills like our survival depends on it. That's who he is. Constant and focused, never distracted by glory or rest.

He was the first commander I ever chose—and he's still the best decision I've made as king. I trust him with my life, and more importantly, I trust him with the lives of those I love.

He's never wanted power, and that's how I know he won't misuse it. When the time comes for him to lead Vaeloria, alongside Annabel, he will do so with the same quiet strength that's carried him this far.

Annabel… she's different from anyone I expected Ryker to draw close to. She's not loud. She's not bold. She speaks softly and only when there's something worth saying.

But she *sees* the people.

And I've seen the way she watches Ryker when he isn't looking. The way Annabel listens to every word he says, even when he's only giving commands to the guard. She has a gentleness Ryker doesn't—an ease that balances his edge. And in turn, I've noticed how he softens, just slightly, when she's near.

Not enough for most to notice, but I know him better than anyone.

They've been spending more time together since the wedding. When we host council dinners, I always find them seated at the same end of the table. She speaks more when he's beside her. He watches the room, but his hand always rests close to hers, as if ready to draw her behind him if danger appears.

I don't think either of them fully understands what's happening between our two kingdoms, but I see it clearly. As Max's father grows older, the need for strong, steady hands to guide Vaeloria becomes more urgent. Ryker and Annabel will rise together.

But even with that reassurance, something else stays heavy in my chest.

Morgathra's coven.

Since the curse broke, they've gone quiet. No movement, messengers, strange omens, or twisted trees in scorched fields.

Nothing. And I don't know what to make of it.

The witches who followed Morgathra were not from these lands. They were exiles, displaced and bitter, loyal to their own causes.

Silence from that kind of enemy rarely means peace. It's not something I don't speak about, and I haven't even brought it up to Max. She's focused on rebuilding—on learning how to be queen, on blending her ways with ours. The last thing she needs is another shadow following her into every chamber.

But Ryker knows, without me saying a word. I see it in the way he's adjusted the guard rotations. The way he keeps an eye on the horizon. The way his hand goes to the hilt of his blade when there's an unseasonably sharp gust of wind.

We're both watching–and waiting.

Whatever comes, we'll be ready. And when the time comes to place a crown on Ryker's head, he'll accept it with the same calm steel he's shown me since the beginning.

THE EMERALD COAST STRETCHES WIDE AND OPEN, WITH GREEN CLIFFS spilling into crashing turquoise waves. Towering stone spires rise from the edge of the kingdom—my kingdom, my home. And now, hers.

We arrive just past dusk, the sky painted in lavender and gold. Torches flicker to life, casting dancing shadows along the palace walls, and the gates swing open as if the kingdom itself is exhaling in relief. The crowd erupts in cheers, of congratulations and heartfelt gratitude that we are home safe.

I wear my ebony cloak, and Max walks beside me in her travel leathers, hair tousled by the wind, no crown on her head. She doesn't wave like a queen. She moves among them like a friend returning home.

The women and children are drawn to her like a tide to the moon. Little ones dart forward with flowers or shy smiles, and she kneels to meet them eye to eye, never rushing, never looking away. The women watch her with something like wonder—this queen without pretense, all strength and grace woven together. And the men… seem to respect her—not because she demands it, but because she's earned it as my queen.

In the days that follow, I help her settle in—not just to the palace, but to the rhythm of the land. I take her flying along the cliff ridges and show her where the waves sing when the moon is high. I walk her through the library, the gardens, and the war hall carved into the mountainside. She asks questions I don't expect and seems to remember everything.

Max spends her mornings with the court scholars, learning our laws and listening to the old stories. She trains with my guard in the afternoons, earning bruises and respect in equal measure.

Sometimes, she runs with the wind at night, her wolf form slipping through the edge of the forest near the cliffs where the mist rises in low, silver curls. I shift and fly above her, just to watch her move.

They said a match like ours was impossible. Dragon and wolf. Fire and instinct. But when I look at her—laughing barefoot in the meadow, running along the coastline, or asleep beside me with her head on my chest and her hand curled over my heart—I understand what they couldn't.

The bond between us isn't something I can explain. It isn't just love; it's deeper than blood, older than magic, and I feel her in my bones. When she's near, the fire in me settles. She's the only creature in all the realms who's ever quieted my inner storm.

Each night, I fall asleep with her in my arms, the sound of the sea crashing on the rocks outside our window and the steady rhythm of her breath against my skin.

She belongs here, as queen of the Emerald Coast.

As my mate.

And if the old world couldn't imagine a time where dragons and wolves ruled side by side—then the old ways will change.

We're building something new, stronger, and ours.

EPILOGUE

MAXIANA

ONE YEAR LATER

The salty air drifts softly through the open windows of our chamber, carrying the scent of sea and pine, wild and fresh. Moonlight spills across the stone floor, catching on the scattered toys my son left behind, tiny wooden dragons, and wolves.

I lie in bed next to him, where he sleeps half-curled like a wolf pup. His tiny fingers twitch, and I swear I can feel the pulse of ancient power mixed with untamed instinct in his breath. He is ours, wolf, dragon, and witch all tangled into one perfect soul.

Kael traces delicate circles along his soft skin. "Look at him," he says, voice thick with something like awe. "Our little Lykos."

Life here on the Emerald Coast is nothing like the life I once knew. I used to be trapped behind my castle walls at all times, my father afraid of the danger of Morgathra's spell. Here, the dragons of Starfall protect us, and we live wild and free.

Kael and I walk through the villages often, watching our people grow into something new, something better. The great stone houses stand tall and proud, no longer shadows of fear but beacons of hope. The air buzzes with magic, but it's gentle now, healing instead of harming.

My father, still strong and steady, rules Ebonclaw with the wisdom and the strength of a lifetime of battles. He visits often, his deep voice carrying the same calm authority that earned him respect long before I met Kael. Watching him and Kael speak together—Alpha and Dragon King—I see a future where our two worlds are bound forever.

My father was never the kind of man to babble or coo, not even when I was small. His love was quieter, albeit incredibly protective, an ever-steady presence in the storm. But when he holds Lykos, something gentler edges into his expression.

He calls him "little wolf," even though the boy's eyes glow like dragon fire, and his laugh comes out in bursts of magic that make the ocean ripple.

Father teaches Lykos how to track with his nose and how to listen to the whispers in the wind. How to stand tall, even when you're small. Lykos mimics him when they spar in the grass, puffing out his chest like he's already a warrior. And my father? He plays along. The same man who once ruled with iron discipline now lets himself be tackled to the ground by a boy with too-big eyes and untamed curls.

Lykos brings out a side of my father I never imagined. And in return, my father grounds him in the strength of his roots—Ebonclaw pride, ancient and unshakable. Dragon fire might live in my son's chest, but it's the steady beat of wolf loyalty that keeps his feet on the ground.

And as I watch them laugh together, two generations apart but bound by something deeper than blood, I realize that maybe this was always meant to be, not just for me and Kael, but for all of us.

I'm learning to rule alongside Kael, and some days it is difficult. The responsibilities weigh heavy, but Kael's hand in mine steadies every step. We balance each other, the wildness in me tempered by his steady fire, his power softened by my instincts. Together, we've built a home where our son can grow strong and free.

With Kael by my side and the sound of our son's breathing filling the room, I dare to believe in something brighter. Our boy is the first of a new kind—the union of wolf, dragon, and witch blood. His magic hums softly, unpredictable and wild, but full of promise.

Kael brushes a stray lock of hair from my face. "Whatever he chooses, he'll have the strength of both our worlds," he says quietly. "And the love to carry it."

I reach for Kael's hand, squeezing it tightly. "We've come so far. From vines strangling Vaeloria to this—peace, family, hope."

He nods, "And we'll protect it, no matter what comes."

The future is ours to shape, and yet, the calm we enjoy here on the Emerald Coast feels almost fragile—like a delicate thread stretched taut between the past and what might come. Morgathra and her coven have stayed silent in our lands. There's no sign of their twisted magic creeping into the forests, no blackened skies, no unnatural storms. For that, I am grateful every day. But the peace we have now isn't a promise it will last forever.

Whispers reach us from the east, carried by travelers and scouts who come to the coast seeking refuge and bringing news. Morgathra's coven has not faded. Instead, they've turned their malice elsewhere, sowing chaos in lands beyond our borders.

I listen carefully to these reports, trying to piece together the fragments of truth from rumor. Villages burned, crops withered, rivers poisoned—places where the witches' dark magic twists nature into something unrecognizable. Mothers whisper warnings to their children, and warriors sharpen blades for battles fought in the haze of fear.

It's a stark reminder that even with her gone, Morgathra's hunger for power hasn't waned. The coven may have been driven into exile but it has only made them more desperate, more dangerous. They want to reclaim what they lost, or perhaps take even more.

Kael watches me closely when I speak of this. His eyes, usually calm and steady, darken with the weight of unspoken worries. "They've chosen to leave our shores—for now," he says, his voice low. "But that doesn't mean they won't return."

I nod, knowing he's right. The dragons and wolves who guard our lands have grown stronger, more united. But even their strength has limits. We've rebuilt Vaeloria and the Emerald Coast, stitched the land back together with stone and magic, but the scars remain, reminders of how fragile peace truly is.

In the quiet moments, I wonder what kind of ruler our son might become. I vow to teach him to use his power wisely, to be the kind of leader who protects rather than conquers.

Kael squeezes my hand, pulling me from my thoughts. "We'll prepare," he says, as sure as the tide's pull. "We will face whatever storms may come."

"So long as we stand together," I whisper, "nothing can break us."

There's comfort in that certainty, in the bond between us and the strength of our people. But I know the road ahead will not be easy. The witches' shadows linger, stretching like a dark tide waiting to crash down.

Night falls gently over the Emerald Coast, wrapping the palace in soft blue shadows and the hush of waves far below. Kael lies beside me, one arm draped over my waist, the other cradling our son, his chest rising and falling with the slow rhythm of sleep. Lykos is nestled between us, small and warm, his little hand wrapped around a lock of my hair, his breathing light and steady.

I should be asleep, too, but I linger in that tender space between waking and dreaming. The hearth embers glow low, casting flickering light across the floor. My body is tired in the best possible way, worn down by love, laughter, and the easy joy of a day spent chasing a toddling baby through the halls of the castle.

Eventually, sleep takes me.

And I dream.

In the dream, Lykos is no longer a baby.

He stands tall—broad-shouldered and sure, with hair the color of flame-kissed gold, eyes like glowing emeralds, and a crown resting lightly on his brow.

All around him, banners ripple in the wind, and it smells of spring. Dragon banners and wolf sigils fly. Even the ancient symbols of the witches are restored–golden, reborn. He walks among a crowd that stretches farther than I can see. The people cheer when he passes, their voices full of hope, not fear.

He is more than a prince now. Even more than even an Alpha King. He is something old made new—fire and fang, moonlight and magic.

I watch as he ascends marble steps to a raised platform at the heart of a great city I've never seen before. The architecture sings with a harmony of cultures: curved archways carved like dragon wings, high towers woven with vines and living flowers, and crystal lanterns pulsing with energy and light. The city is alive, breathing, a place that has no memory of war.

Lykos turns to address the gathered nations. He speaks in a deep voice, calm and steady like Kael's, but edged with the quiet, sharp confidence of my father. Words I can't fully understand ring through the square, and yet, I feel the meaning of them in my bones. Peace. Unity. Renewal.

He's not alone.

Annabel and Ryker stand nearby—older, wiser, weathered by time but unbroken. Ryker holds a staff marked with the crest of Ebonclaw. Annabel's hand rests lightly on his arm, her eyes kind and fierce.

Dragons hover in the skies above the city, their wings outstretched like guardians. Wolves gather on the forested cliffs beyond the city walls, howling not in warning, but in celebration. Witches walk freely among the people, heads high, magic sparkling from their fingertips like shooting stars.

This is not a dream of war or darkness.

This is a vision of what comes after.

Of what we are building.

Lykos lowers his head in solemn reverence then raises his hand. Magic ripples outward from his palm—blazing fire, roaring wind, bright threads of something ancient and holy. It flows through the crowd, touching every creature, every spirit. I feel it touch me, too, though I'm only a spirit here. I weep with the beauty of it, of him. Of what he's become.

And then he looks directly at me.

"Mother," he says, and though it's just one word, it breaks something open in my chest. "Thank you."

My breath catches, but I don't have time to answer. The dream world shifts, begins to fold away like a page turning in a great book.

And then I wake.

I blink slowly. The dawn light is just beginning to spill over the windowsill. Kael is still asleep, his brow smooth, lips parted. Lykos is snuggled against his chest, drooling slightly, his chubby hand now resting against Kael's bare skin. He's still small. Still perfect. Still entirely ours.

The room is quiet, except for the rhythmic crash of waves and the distant cry of gulls.

We're home.

Not in a vision of the future or the ruins of the past, but here, now, together.

I brush a kiss across my son's forehead, the dream lingering behind my eyes, but I don't chase it.

This is how it was always meant to end—no battles, crowns, or sacrifices, just love. Love, family and a baby tucked between dragon and wolf, his breath soft and his future wide open.

I close my eyes again, letting sleep find me a second time, holding tight to the sweetness of this moment.

Because we are safe.

We are whole.

And we are exactly where we belong.

Thanks for reading! Book 3, based on Rapunzel, *is coming soon!*

ALSO BY BELLA MOONDRAGON

The Alpha King's Breeder series:
Bought by the Alpha: The Alpha King's Breeder Book 1
Loved by the Alpha: The Alpha King's Breeder Book 2
Lost by the Alpha: The Alpha King's Breeder Book 3
Luna of the Alpha: The Alpha King's Breeder Book 4
Legacy of the Alpha: The Alpha Kings's Breeder Book 5
Daughter of the Alpha: The Alpha King's Breeder Book 6
Descendants of the Alpha: The Alpha King's Breeder Book 7
Shadow of the Alpha: The Alpha King's Breeder Book 8
Son of the Alpha: The Alpha King's Breeder Book 9
Spare of the Alpha: The Alpha King's Breeder Book 10
Claimed by the Alpha: The Alpha King's Breeder Book 11
Atonement for the Alpha King: The Alpha King's Breeder Book 12
Rejected by the Alpha: The Alpha King's Breeder Book 13
Abducted by the Alpha: The Alpha King's Breeder Book 14
Wolf Shifter Fairy Tale Retellings series
Beauty and the Alpha Beast
Sleeping Beasty
Tangling With the Alpha
The Luna's Vampire Prince series:
The Culling
The Kingdom
The Conquered
Pregnant With Four Alphas' Babies
Chosen As the Breeder

Mated to Four Alphas

Threats Against the Breeder

At War for the Breeder

The Stolen Breeder

Four Alphas, Four Babies

Becoming the Luna Queen

Descendants of the Breeder

Desired by the Devil series

Whispers of the Devil

Banter of the Devil

Murmurs of the Devil

The Mafia Kings series

Indebted to the Mafia King

<u>Loved by the Mafia King</u>

Claimed by the Mafia King

Secrets of the Mafia King

Burned by the Mafia King

Kidnapped by the Mafia King (coming soon!)

Dark Stalker Romance series

Tempted by Sin

Fated to Sin

Secret Billionaires series

Finding the Secret Billionaire by Olivia Bhelle Kildare

Falling for My Secret Billionaire by Bella Moondragon

Driven by the Secret Billionaire by ID Johnson

Wolf Shifter Alpha Kings series

Ravens and Ruins

Sundrops and Shadows

Snowflakes and Sabotage

The Vampire King's Feeder series

Claiming the Alpha's Daughter

Loving the Alpha's Daughter

Finding the Alpha's Daughter

Bewitching the Alpha's Son (coming soon!)

Writing as B. Moon

The Boy Who Died

Sign up for Bella's newsletter here.

Or get a free novella from The Alpha King's Breeder series when you sign up here:
The Beta and the Maid

Follow Bella on Facebook here.

Follow Bella on Bookbub here.